I0636416

Dexter S. King

History of the North Russell Street M.E. Church and Sabbath School

with a brief account of St. John's church at the Odeon

Dexter S. King

History of the North Russell Street M.E. Church and Sabbath School
with a brief account of St. John's church at the Odeon

ISBN/EAN: 9783337348076

Printed in Europe, USA, Canada, Australia, Japan

Cover: Foto ©Andreas Hilbeck / pixelio.de

More available books at **www.hansebooks.com**

Transactions of the New England Methodist Historical Society.
No. 2.

HISTORY

OF THE

NORTH RUSSELL STREET

M. E. Church and Sabbath School;

WITH A BRIEF ACCOUNT OF

ST. JOHN'S CHURCH AT THE ODEON.

EDITED BY D. S. KING.

BOSTON:
FOR SALE BY J. P. MAGEE, 5 CORNHILL.
1861.

Printed by
GEO. C. RAND & AVERY, 3 CORNHILL, BOSTON.

ORIGIN OF THE WORK.

PURSUANT to a vote of our teachers, in June last, we instituted measures to prepare and publish a history of the North Russell Street Sabbath School. We had the good fortune to secure the services of one to act as our historian, who has had an extensive knowledge of the school from its commencement, and whose qualifications for the work need no commendation from us.

It was not our original design to refer to the church, beyond what was necessary to the history of the school; but considerations which we need not enumerate here, have led to the production of a history of the church, and of a brief account of the St. John's Church at the Odeon.

To the past and present members of our church and school, the subject matter must be of thrilling interest. For such it has been prepared. And yet we are not without hope that it will be extensively read by others. True, there are some items not of general interest; but as the price is very low, no one need feel that he pays for matter of purely local and personal interest. We think the chapter on "building and finance," might prove a salutary lesson to young societies. The account of the Odeon enterprise is certainly worth the price of the book to any person not familiar with its history. And we are sure that any Sabbath-school teacher, who reads the chapters on "The Means of Interesting the Children," "Education for Usefulness," and "Sacred Memoirs," will be richly repaid.

The name of the editor may appear, to a stranger, of frequent mention on these pages. Our history would not be complete without it, and yet from delicacy, Mr. King has refrained from the use of his own name, where others would have inserted it. It is not for us to amend his work, and yet we take the liberty of saying, that he not only aided as a clergyman, in the organization of the church and school, till the appointment of a pastor, but for the next two years performed the duties of an elder, as our young minister had not been ordained. In issuing this volume, we follow the counsel of the fathers of the church. We sincerely desire that it may prove a blessing to many.

To those who are or have been of our church or school, we especially present our Christian salutations.

J. FRED EASTMAN,	MARIA, E. TUCKER,	*Committee of*
BARZILLAI HINDS,	JULIA A. WHEATON,	*the Sabbath*
A. J. BECKWITH,	SARAH E. LEWIS,	*School.*

PREFACE.

Our original undertaking, as stated by the Committee, was simply a history of the North Russell Street Sabbath School, and, with that alone in view, several articles in that department were prepared. On comparing the statistics, we found that the vicissitudes of the school had been extreme. It seemed hardly fair towards pastors, superintendents, and teachers, to publish these without some explanation as to the causes leading to such results. In preparing what was absolutely necessary for this purpose, we saw more fully the importance of making a permanent record of all the important events in the history of the church. We have given the facts with brevity, leaving our readers to be self-taught from the lessons which they suggest. The Sabbath-school history is written with more fulness. This seems appropriate, as the whole is published by the school, and as any suggestions there made are designed for the more youthful of our readers.

The most delicate part of our work has been to prepare the " Sacred Memoirs." We have no fear of the charge that we have said too much of any one, but it may be thought we should have written notices of others. Under some circumstances we would do it most gladly. But our limited space will confine us to the original design, of writing only of such as had been members of the Sabbath School, and had acquired distinction by long and faithful service as teachers, or eminence in the cause by some other means. Christian worthies have gone from this to the church triumphant, and good·teachers from the school to heaven, whose memoirs are not included in our plan. If any one has been unjustly omitted, the responsibility must rest upon others. The Committee issued a sufficient number of circulars, asking for facts and suggestions; but the returns were few and meagre, with five or six exceptions. These remarks will apply in relation to other matters on which we sought information.

It has been no light task to collect all our facts. They have been received by piece-meal, and the history has been written in scraps, at odd hours. These considerations may be some apology for any want of perfect arrangement, or for literary defect. The subject matter is highly interesting, and having done the best we could under the circumstances, we make our humble bow.

The chapter on St. John's Church, was prepared entirely on our own judgment. It has been approved by several gentlemen connected with that church, as well as by a Committee (Messrs. E. Otheman and E. O. Haven) of the New England Methodist Historical Society. We hope it will be acceptable to that noble Christian band, and, by reviving reminiscences of happy associations, bring fresh delight to their souls.

THE EDITOR.

BOSTON, January 22, 1861.

HISTORY.

CHAPTER I.

INTRODUCTION.

At the recent celebration occasioned by the placing of the Webster Statue in the grounds of our State House, the late Rev. Dr. Sanger entered into conversation with a gentleman by his side. Hon. Edward Everett was to deliver the oration. As was natural on such an occasion, the venerable Doctor related an incident of his college life. He said: " At the commencement of my Senior year at Harvard, a very intelligent and interesting lad of about fourteen years of age came to me and said that as he must submit to the rules of drudgery, he should like to be my fag and be under my protection. I was much pleased with his appearance, felt complimented by the confidence he placed in me, and I accepted his offer. The year passed away without my calling upon him for a single service. The offensive custom is abolished now, but it was imperative then. It is a pleasant reflection that I did not avail myself of my privileges, and the more so as that boy was Edward Everett."

The emotions of that hour were an ample compensation for all the indulgence granted. And yet this was one of the little events in the good man's life, and was related as such. He had far higher delight in the recollection of noble acts which had required toil and sacrifice.

How exalted would be the feelings of the teacher who took Morrison to the Sabbath School, could he now look upon the work which Morrison has done. If Peter Böhler could look upon the world as it now is, he might find the earthly vessel too weak to contain the joy he would feel for having instructed John Wesley in the doctrine of salvation by faith.

While the luxury of doing good is an instant reward, while the promise of a heavenly inheritance to the faithful inspires delightful anticipations, the retrospect on labors of love makes a feast to the soul, and it may be enjoyed at pleasure. As the old soldier who has endured hardships and encountered dangers upon the battle-field with success for liberty, loves

" To fight his battles o'er again,"

so the Christian hero is inspired with abundant gratitude and joy, when, after years of toil, he is permitted to witness a successful result of his labors. Thus, happily, as years increase upon us, the pleasure of recollection becomes one of the most delightful sources of enjoyment to those who have consecrated their talents to the service of God, and for the happiness of their fellow-creatures.

That those who sowed in this field as pioneers may know what fruit has been gathered; that others may be inspired with the hope of success; that a reliable record may descend to posterity, and that the riches of grace may be declared to the glory of God, we publish a history of the North Russell Street Church and Sabbath School.

CHAPTER II.

In 1833, the only Methodist churches in Boston and the immediate vicinity were those at Bennet and Bromfield streets, one at East Cambridge, and one in Charlestown, and all of these had been established quite a number of years. About this time the house on Church Street was purchased from an unsuccessful society. Abel Stevens was stationed there two years; he was ably supported by the church, and the result was a decided success. In 1836 a small band of brethren sustained preaching in a hall in South Boston.

The next movement was for a church at the "West End." Albert H. Brown, fresh from the victory at Church Street, and D. S. King, who had spent several years in "breaking up new ground" in the Conference, took the lead in the matter. In the autumn of 1836 they searched that part of the city very thoroughly for a suitable place for preaching. There was no hall to be had. The only eligible room was in the Wells School House, on Blossom Street, and this, by the aid of influential brethren in the several churches, was procured.

The school-room was free of rent; preaching was to be supplied gratuitously till the next session of the Conference; expenses, of course, would be trifling; no effort was therefore made to enlist a company for the undertaking, and the cause was left, in this respect, to the ruling of Providence. Public notice was given that Abel Stevens, pastor of Bennet Street Church, would preach the opening sermon, Sabbath morning, Jan. 22, 1837. Mr. Stevens was enthusiastic in behalf of the new enterprise, and in commending it from his pulpit expressed the hope that many of his people would embark in it.

The appointed time arrived, and with it came a violent snow-storm, but the preacher and a good congregation were present.

The pleasures of the first service were in glorious contrast with the darkening clouds and stormy blasts without.

The preachers in and about Boston generously contributed their services. Father Taylor, for one, preached to a crowded audience, conferring his sanction and benediction.

About twenty persons immediately banded together and held prayer and class meetings regularly, though they continued their membership with their respective churches for months afterwards. In purpose and effort they were the same as if regularly organized.

They had an elder, a member of the New England Conference with them, and very soon had received a goodly number of probations. Charles and Relief L. Woodbury united in February, and were the first. Eliza A. Saunders (now Mrs. Sam'l Adams), Abigail Houghton, Mary J. Houghton, Sarah Callum, Elizabeth W. Newhall, and Betsey Ramsdell joined in June; Lucy Rice, Hannah Alexander, Lydia Taylor (now Mrs. Rodney Eastman), Rebecca Nutting, and Nancy Spurr, in July; Jeremiah Gale, Calvin G. Jones, and Eliza Dexter, in August.

At the Conference, Moses L. Scudder was stationed preacher in charge. He was a young man, then having preached only a few months after leaving the Wesleyan University. He preached his first sermon as pastor, June 18, 1837.

Between this date and the 29th of August, when the first Quarterly Conference was held and the church fully organized, the following named persons presented certificates of membership, which we give in alphabetical order. Sam'l Adams, Albert H. Brown, Benj. H. Barnes, Eunice S. Beverly, Catharine F. Bosworth, Noah Childs, Ann Childs, Harriet A. Clapp, Isaac J. P. Collyer, Susan Clark, Augustus Dawley, Mary Dawley, Rebecca Douglas, Sam'l W. Edwards, Wm. C. Evans, Harriet W. Fabyan, Anthony French, Eveline French, Josiah S. Gale, Mary Giddings, Charlotte Green, Phineas Howes, Sarah C. Harding, Loenza Houghton, Mary Huntoon, Hannah E. Haley, Louis S. Jones, Abigail Lakeman, Matilda Lewis, ·Elizabeth Lakeman, Elizabeth Moses, Ezra Mudge, Hannah B. Mudge, Mary Merritt, Harum Merrill, Diana Merrill, Lydia

Pike, Thomas Patten, Jr., Mary L. Puffer, Elizabeth Potter, Thomas W. Quimby, Betsey Robey, Penninnah Robey, Elizabeth Robey, Reuben Roberts, Jane Roberts, Wm. Simonds, Sarah Skinner, Lucy Spear, Ebenezer Thompson, Hannah Thompson, Hannah M. Thompson, Charles Taylor, Susanna Temple, Mary Trench, Alexander Wilson, Mary Watkins, Hannah Weeks, Emeline Whipple, Phebe R. Young, and Mary Ann Young. ·Of these, 61 in all, 30 were from Bennet Street Church, 16 from Bromfield Street, 4 from Church Street, and the others from out of the city. Adding the 16 on probation, we organized with 77 members in Society. We should be disposed to distinguish the names of the very first "about twenty" persons who composed the original band, but we have no list of their names. The greater part of them are, however, indicated by the Sabbath School organization.

Mr. Scudder remained two years with the Society. He commenced preaching in the new house in January, 1839. He left the church and school in a prosperous condition.

Jefferson Hascall succeeded Mr. Scudder the next two years, and the work of grace continued during the whole term. In the winter of 1839-40 the interest was intense. It was thought that more than two hundred persons were converted who had been to the altar, many of them on the spot. Some of them were stout-hearted men, who had long withstood the influences of the church, but here they were constrained to yield. A large number of the converts belonged to other congregations, and some to other denominations. They came here to be blest, and returned to their homes to be useful. Not one half of the converts united with this church, nor were they expected to do so. The revival commenced here, but it soon spread to many of the churches in the city. It may be proper to say that a pleasing and gradual work had been for a long time in progress in this church, but the immediate cause of a work so powerful was owing to peculiar circumstances. We had just heard of the burning of the steamer Lexington. Almost every person had lost a friend or acquaintance. A heavy cloud of gloom hung over the whole city. A series of meetings was in progress at this church at the time, and President Mahan was associated with the pastor in the labors of the pulpit. People literally flocked to the altar, as clouds and as doves to their windows: On the first opportunity the altar and several pews were immediately filled. The freedom with which venerable men of other Christian names led their sons to the place of consecration will be long remembered. The scenes witnessed in those meetings, if portrayed by a skilful writer, would be of thrilling interest.

Charles K. True was the preacher for the next two years. The first was a year of great prosperity; but during his second year there commenced a retrogression in the Society, which seemed beyond the control of pastor or people.

CHAPTER III

SOME of the causes of this reversion are easily understood. The most prominent was, that about this time conversions ceased almost entirely, not only in this church, but in all the churches in the city. Why this was, it is not so easy to tell. Some attributed it to the influence of the doctrines taught by William Miller and others, that the second coming of Christ would take place early in 1843. This, we have no doubt, had its influence in the matter, as many persons were unduly excited on the subject, while other sincere believers in the doctrine were calm as the summer morning. So far as this church was concerned, we think that Millerism, so called, did not produce a cessation of the revival. There were a few excellent members who embraced the doctrine, but they did not obtrude their views improperly in the meetings, and we are not aware that more than one member of this church suffered spiritual loss in consequence of this faith. That was a person of great firmness of character, large conscientiousness, and an entire sincerity, which was evinced by a rigid determination to sell his possessions and give all to the poor, and we have no doubt he would have done it, but for an injunction which he could not resist. This person made no trouble with the church, but withdrew and enjoyed his liberty with others of like faith,— the ultra Adventists. We are aware that some churches did have trouble with some of their members, on account of this faith, and perhaps through the imprudence of both parties. At the same time, we are of opinion that others were not in the least affected by it. The Adventists were principally in congregations by themselves, and were in numbers a "feeble folk," when compared with the aggregate Christian body of the city. So while we admit that the Adventists contributed their share of influence to this result, we cannot falsify history by charging the principal cause to them. A more important consideration is, that from ten to fifteen years the churches of different denominations had had an abundance of " four days," or " protracted meetings," and employed many speakers of the most powerful gifts in exhortation and persuasion, and in the latter part of this period the services of Messrs. Mahan, Maffitt, Knapp, and others had been brought into requisition. Under their influence religious interest gained a high culminating point, a position not long sustained. The result was, that while stable Christians were less ardent, some who were not well established " fell away," and the unconverted, generally, seemed to lose their convictions. The usual means of grace did not produce the same results as formerly, and we presume there were but few conversions for several years, excepting through direct and personal effort, and the number of such was not large. Whether such revivals are more or less beneficial than a steady work of grace, it is not our province to say; and if it were, we are incompetent to decide.

But we must return from this digression. The effects of this general cause were fully shared by this church. And there were yet other circumstances that bore heavily against its prosperity.

About the first of January, 1842, the Odeon was opened for Methodist preaching, and for reasons elsewhere stated, the undertaking was approved by our leading men. The pastor commended the enterprise, and encouraged the people to embark in it. Forty persons went by certificate, besides some other members of the congregation. As a whole, it was an interesting class of members. One half of them were men. Of the number were Francis Childs, Milton Gale, J. Wesley Griswold, Augustus Lothrop, Amos B. Merrill, Calvin S. Magoun, Samuel S. Soden, George C. Rand, and Alexander Wilson. After the tide turned against the church, the loss of these members was severely felt in the social meetings and in the financial interest.

Houserents were then high at the West End, and while some families moved out of town, some went to other parts of the city, and having no accessions by conversion the congregation became small.

The debt upon the church was heavy, and the interest must be paid. Reckoning the interest with current expenses, the demand for assessments was alarming. Some people had no fancy for this part of the means of grace, and such newcomers to town did not present their certificates to this church.

The house of worship which had answered the purpose very well when all went to church to see the salvation of God, and did see it, would not compare well with other churches in the city, and of itself was not an attractive place.

All these unpropitious circumstances, gathering cloud upon cloud, produced an obscurity which could be pierced only by the eye of faith.

We have mentioned 1843 as the time of their commencement. They were comparatively small at first, but they continued for several years, growing with our decrease, and strengthening with our weakness.

The membership appears by the statistics to have remained about the same in numbers during the two succeeding years, while George Landon was pastor; but it appears that a considerable number of whom he had hope, were not considered worth counting by his successor. They had left without a certificate. We mean no reflection. Mr. Landon, and also the other preachers who shared with the church the hardships of those times, were requested for a second year's service.

William H. Hatch was stationed there in 1845 and 1846. The membership at the close of these years was at a low figure for numbers.

The alternative of having a better house of worship, or of giving up the whole concern, had been fixed upon, with a very decided expectation, however, that the cause would not be abandoned. Aside from the usual duties of the pastor, Mr. Hatch did effective service by way of raising funds for building purposes. The church was built, as elsewhere stated.

During the next two years, Wm. Rice being the preacher, the increase of church members was thirty-five. About this number were converted, and added to the church as probationers during the two years. As the most of them joined during the last half of Mr. Rice's second year, their names (many of them valuable here or elsewhere) will appear as having joined the church in full connection the next year. And we will take this opportunity of saying that throughout this history the probationers have been enumerated as members of the church. We had of necessity to take some of the statistics from the General Minutes, where no distinction was made till 1849, and for the sake of uniformity we have not made it where we might have done it. This fact will in part account for the large diminution of numbers in 1843, as many probationers of the previous year were "dropped." A large majority of them, however, united with the church in full connection, and many of them are now distinguished members of the church in different places. So the principal cause lies in removal by certificate.

Mark Trafton was stationed here the next two years. During the first year of his pastorate the increase of members was twenty-two. The second year there was an essential falling off by certificate. In justice to Mr. Trafton, it should be stated that by previous arrangement with the church and the bishop, he spent a considerable part of the year in Europe.

These last eight years were a season of heavy burden-bearing. How the interest on the debt, and the current expenses were paid, we were about to say no man can tell, and yet it is not so. The noble subscriptions of all the men of larger means (the number was small), of the young men, and of the young ladies who toiled for their daily bread, will not be soon forgotten.

It was the faith of the church that the time to favor our Zion, temporally and spiritually, had now come. N. E. Cobleigh was the preacher for the next two years. The church was increased by nearly one hundred members, and the Sabbath School was enlarged in proportion. Of the financial success we shall speak elsewhere.

J. Augustus Adams was stationed with us at the Conference of 1853, and remained two years. There were some conversions and some removals. The numbers underwent a slight diminution.

Moses A. Howe was the next pastor, for one year. Unfortunately for him, and for the church, it was to him a year of severe family affliction. A protracted typhoid fever prostrated him for the greater part of what is considered the "working season," and for many weeks he could benefit the church only by showing them how happy a man in physical distress could be. Mr. Howe began to regain his strength previous to the session of Conference, but he was not returned, because it was feared that he might not be physically adequate to the services required. Happily, however, the result proved this a miscalculation. The spiritual condition of the church was good.

There were some removals during Mr. Howe's pastorate, but not enough to seriously affect the numbers in the membership. And yet, in reality, the church had suffered extensively by the few removals of the last three years. A majority of the men of more ample means had left by certificate. About three fifths of the financial strength in the official board had been lost in those years. How to support a preacher was a problem. Bishop Janes very kindly, and not less wisely, sent one of our own "boys" to stay up the hands and to encourage the hearts of the "old folks at home," and to retrieve their fortunes. Persons outside of the board, and not of the membership, rallied with unusual energy to our financial support; the congregation was enlarged; a pleasant revival was enjoyed, adding about thirty probationers; and the finances were managed without embarrassment. The state of Mr. Studley's health seemed to render a change of climate of vast importance to him. At the same time, having a call to take charge of a new church, with flattering prospects and in a genial climate, there seemed to be an opening and intimation of Providence. At the close of one year he was transferred to the New York Conference by Bishop Baker, and was stationed in Brooklyn. The church approved, and yet deeply regretted, the removal.

Henry W. Warren was the next preacher. He remained two years. A part of the time he was Superintendent of the Sabbath School. The church had an increase of fifty members, and the school prospered during his pastorate.

J. W. Dadmun was the next and the present pastor. Thus far peace and prosperity have attended his labors. The increase of membership has been fifty-five. Seventy probationers have been received, — forty of whom were members of the Sabbath School. Under his auspices congregational singing has been successfully instituted in the place of choir singing. May the future weeks of his service here be as the past, and much more abundant.

CHAPTER IV

QUARTERLY CONFERENCES. — The first Quarterly Meeting Conference for this station was held at the house of Ezra Mudge, August 29, 1837. Members: Barthlomew Otheman, P. E.; Moses L. Scudder, preacher in charge; D. S. King, Sup. Leaders: Ezra Mudge, A. H. Brown, Ebenezer Thompson, Noah Childs, B. H. Barnes, and Thos. Patten, Jr., Secretary. Ezra Mudge, A. H. Brown, Augustus Dawley, Noah Childs, and Anthony French were, at this meeting, elected Stewards.

Since this organization the following persons have been appointed Leaders: Samuel Adams, 1837; I. J. P. Collyer, Franklin Rand, 1838; John Converse, J. B. Holman, Milton Gale, Harum Merrill, A. P. Battey, D. S. King, 1839; Joshua Dunbar, Thomas Moses, E. S. Norris, 1840; Andrew Brown, Benjamin Welch, Jr., J. Wesley Griswold, James Hamlet, J. C. Ricker, Eli F. Southard, Joseph H. Osgood, Arnold W. McClure, 1841; John H. Collins, Charles Waite, 1843; Barzillai Hinds, 1846; Seth Whittier, 1849; L. L. Tarbell, 1851; Joseph H. Tucker, 1852; Wm. Blakemore, John H. Thurber, Cornelius Hamblin, 1853; Thos. N. Chase, Winslow S. Kyle, 1855; Rodney Eastman, 1856; Andrew Pike, William Pearson, 1857; Sidney Hatch, Wm. Light, J. Fred. Eastman, 1858; Joseph Sawyer, 1860.

The Stewards, who have been since elected, are: Franklin Rand, 1838; Charles Woodbury, Reuben H. Sawin, 1839; Albert F. Brown, 1840; Chas. B. Rice, John Russell, Milton Gale, Wymond Bradbury, 1841; John H. Collins, Samuel Adams, 1842: Nathaniel Carr, 1843; Thomas G. Rounds, 1844; Horace S. Favor, Milton A. Straw, 1845; J. C. Hackett, 1846; Jeremiah Litch, 1847; Sylvanus W. Robinson, 1848; Jabez Pratt, J. B. Hamblin, 1850; Hiram Fuller, 1851; Russell J. Parker, 1855; Joel Snow, 1856; Edward A. Johnson, Andrew J. Hall, 1857; Daniel W. Gardner, 1858; Thilman Warren, 1859; Daniel W. Russell, John S. Damrell, 1860.

Additional members as preachers besides the pastors: R. D. Easterbrook, superannuated preacher. Edward Otheman, and Moses A. Howe, located; Daniel Wise, Ichabod Marcy, I. J. P. Collyer, E. S. Norris, J. B. Holman, Wm. H. Woodbury, Walker Booth, Elijah Brigham, Wm. S. Studley, George Dunbar, Jacob Boyce, James C. Pearce, Francis Metcalf, Joseph R. Carr, and Thomas Freeman, Local Preachers.

The Presiding Elders have been Bartholomew Otheman, David Kilburn, Thomas C. Peirce, Phineas Crandall, James Porter, Edward Otheman, and Loranus Crowell.

Secretaries of the Conference: Thomas Patten, Jr., the first four years regularly; John H. Collins, full one half of the last twenty years; L. L. Tarbell, and Wm. Blakemore, several years each; and Russell J. Parker, several successive quarters; J. B. Holman, E. S. Norris, E. Mudge, D. S. King, Alden Avery, and J. C. Pearce have served occasionally.

Treasurers of the Board of Stewards: Albert H. Brown, Franklin Rand, Samuel Adams, Wm. Blakemore, and William Pearson.

BOARD OF TRUSTEES. — The act to incorporate the "Associate Trustees of the Methodist Religious Society in Boston," was approved by Gov. Everett, March 28, 1838. It was granted to Ezra Mudge, Albert H. Brown, Lemuel Tompkins, and their associates. The first meeting was held April 17, 1839, at which time Dexter S. King, John Gove, Benjamin H. Barnes, Thomas Patten, Jr., and Freeman M. Dyer were elected associates, and the eight trustees thus constituted signed a declaration of acceptance in the book of records.

The Trustees since elected have been Charles Woodbury, E. S. Norris, 1840; John H. Collins and J. C. Hackett, 1843; Jeremiah Litch, 1847; Seth Whittier and George Russell, 1849; Joseph B. Hamblin, 1852; Wm. Blakemore, 1855; Joel Snow, 1857.

The Presidents have been Ezra Mudge, D. S. King, George Russell, and Wm. Blakemore.

Treasurers: Albert H. Brown, John Gove, and Charles Woodbury. Mr. Woodbury has served the last eleven years.

Secretaries: Thomas Patten, Jr., to 1847; John H. Collins from then to the present time.

J. C. Hackett has been the Auditor for many years.

CHAPTER V.

THE building of a church edifice was early contemplated. At the first Quarterly Conference, Aug 27, 1837, " a committee of seven was appointed from the several churches to carry forward a plan of operations with regard to erecting a new church in this part of the city, consisting of Ezra Mudge and A. H. Brown, Blossom Street ; Isaac Rich, B. H. Barnes, and John Gove, Bennet Street ; Wm. M. True, Bromfield Street, and Freeman M. Dyer, Church Street ; and the committee is to report as to prospects and means."

The Quarterly Conference, Feb. 26, 1838, voted " That it is the sense of this Conference that a free church be built on the land purchased by the Associate Board of Trustees, agreeable to the economy of the Methodist Episcopal Church." This was previous to the act of incorporation, and we believe the Board of Trustees was more an anticipated fact than a reality. Further, the land had not then been deeded to any body. On the first day of the ensuing month, A. H. Brown and John Gove purchased in their own right, but in behalf of the Society, the land where the church and the dwelling-houses in front of it stand. At this time neither " the sense " of the Quarterly Conference, or of the " committee of seven," had discovered the " means." The estate was bought in anticipation of what *might* be. It was a good investment to be kept as it was. There were 8801½ feet of land, with three dwelling-houses thereon, at $1.25 per foot, costing $11,001.66.

Some time during the succeeding summer it was decided to *commence* building a house of worship, to consist, for the present, of a little more than what is now the vestry, for an audience-room, with one class-room on each side of the entrance ; and over the front part of this story a Conference and

Sabbath-School room. This was to be a temporary matter till we could build a church such as we now have.

Building to this extent was ventured upon, not because the Society had the means to pay for it, for it required a heavy draft upon the ability of the members to meet the current expenses, but because a necessity was upon them. The school-room was too small; they could have it only for Sabbath morning and afternoon services. As God was crowning their labors by the conversion of many souls, they thought the other churches would come to their aid. They expected to make some profit on the estate just mentioned, as two dwelling-houses were to be left standing, and then to leave ample passage-way to the church.

And last, but very important, Sereno Fisk, of Billerica, now of Kenosha, Wis., proposed to loan the Society $15,000 to aid the enterprise, and intimated that he might eventually donate a part of the amount. Ten thousand dollars of the amount was received. The whole of the original design was not carried out. It should be kept in lasting remembrance and with the most profound gratitude to Mr. Fisk, that he did make the Society a present of five thousand dollars. This was given soon after the property came into the possession of the trustees, and was the only subscription applied to the original building, with the exception of $428.35, subscribed in small sums, " to finish the church," the records say. We think the subscription was to furnish it, and that it was so applied. The northeast corner-stone was laid with appropriate services, Oct. 12, 1838. In it was deposited a box containing several valuable publications, and a document prepared by the pastor, which may reveal to some future generation mighty deeds and worthy names, which shall have been long forgotten.

The church was consecrated Jan. 15, 1839, in a manner quite novel.

The usual sermon was omitted. Several prayers were offered, a number of addresses made, and the whole was interspersed with congregational singing. The gentlemen who took part in the exercises were the men for the work, and they were prepared to do it well. The house was packed; the people were interested and blessed. We never witnessed the dedication of a house of worship where the services were more appropriate, or where the people were more delighted.

The house was built by Messrs. Brown and Gove upon their own pecuniary responsibility, but for the church.

On the 18th of April, 1839, Messrs. Brown and Gove conveyed to the associate trustees the land, dwelling-houses, church, and furniture, at first cost, $18,865.29, after having deducted the subscription of $428.35. This became the debt of the church. The interest on this amount being $1,131, it was to be met by rent of two houses and the cellar under the church, $675, leaving $456 to be appropriated from pew rents. This was not a very dark prospect to men who were pressing on from victory to victory, but it has since been seen from a stand-point where all its horrors were revealed.

In the spring of 1846, the affairs of the Society and the condition of the meeting-house had become such, that evidently they must be improved or abandoned. We have referred to the circumstances elsewhere. A church must be had at any rate, if we continued a people. It could not be built without foreign aid. The debts of the Society amounted to about $14,000. The "Wesleyan Chapel Fund Society" voted to assume the floating debt, — all except the mortgage; the subscribers to the cause having the privilege of taking stock in the house. The front land was sold, and our present neat and commodious church was completed. It was dedicated March 19, 1847. The sermon was preached by Abel Stevens. Of course it was able and interesting. As a part of the exercises, the following original hymn, by John H. Collins, was sung by the choir and congregation in the tune of Old Hundred.

> O Thou whose name is ever praised
>   In realms above, o'er earth and sea,
> This temple, to thine honor raised,
>   We consecrate, with joy, to thee.

Here condescend thy name to place ;
Thy glory in this house display :
Here, Lord, unveil thy smiling face,
And guard this flock from error's sway.

Give wisdom to thy servants, Lord,
Who in this desk thy heralds stand ;
With power divine, oh, clothe the word,
Inspire the tongue, and stay the hand.

Let fire upon this altar burn,
And fervent prayer as incense rise ;
While thousands here their sins shall mourn,
Thou wilt accept the sacrifice.

Here may the choir their anthems raise,
Their harps be ne'er on willows hung ;
Nor here be heard, in chants of praise,
One jarring note, one chord unstrung.

But earthly temples must decay, —
Art's noblest work, how quickly gone !
Our hopes we build, our all we lay
On JESUS CHRIST, the corner-stone.

The land sold for about the price anticipated, but the church cost some $1,600 over the estimated expense, notwithstanding the good judgment and rigid economy of J. C. Hackett, who superintended the work. "The Wesleyan Chapel Fund Society" was a generous youth and meant well, but it could not raise the means ; it paid about fifty per cent. These two mishaps left the Society in debt, after purchasing the organ, about the same as before, fourteen thousand dollars, and four thousand dollars above previous calculations. This was too much, but there was no way to reduce it at that time. The trustees waited in great anxiety for a propitious opportunity.

At length it seemed at hand. Aug. 19, 1852, the trustees "appointed D. S. King and N. E. Cobleigh, the pastor, a committee to raise, if practicable, the sum of $4,000, or an amount sufficient to reduce the debt to ten thousand dollars." The debt was reduced to a sum below that mark. The members of this Society did what they could. No very large amount was asked or received from any one individual. We have not the subscription paper at hand, but can state that the contributions were numerous, by the members of the several Methodist churches in Boston.

We must not omit to mention the benefactions of that prince of church redeemers, Lee Claflin, of the church at large.

The raising of this subscription was no small work. That the honors may be fairly reckoned, it is proper to say that "we" presided, and the rest of the committee raised the money. And while the trustees are very thankful to the donors, they owe Mr. Cobleigh an immense debt of gratitude.

CHAPTER VI.

THE North Russell Street Church had not the honor of originating the Odeon enterprise, and cannot, by pre-eminence, be its historian; but she had an interest in it important to her own record. As there is no account of that undertaking, to which we can refer for a proper understanding of the subject, we find a necessity of saying something about it; and it is done the more freely as we would perpetuate the recollection of one of the most important events in the history of Boston Methodism. For this purpose we shall give a brief account of the origin, progress, and influence of this church. The Odeon building was located on the north corner of Federal and Franklin streets. It had formerly been a theatre. It was hired and occupied by the Boston Academy of Music, and the name of the building made appropriate to their use of it.

However strange it may seem at this time, the location was desirable for a Methodist congregation. Genteel American families resided on Fort Hill, and on nearly all the streets in the vicinity of the Odeon. Dr. Gannett's church was just across the way; a Baptist church, now Dr. Stowe's, stood on the corner of Federal and Milk streets; and a Unitarian congregation occupied the stone church on Purchase Street.

The Odeon was opened for Methodist preaching the first of January, 1842. As we have elsewhere stated, there had been a revival in progress in the Methodist churches in the city for several years. Some of the churches were crowded, and all were well sustained. A new, or larger, field for labor seemed necessary to develop the energies of the church. There was no Methodist congregation in the city proper east of Washington Street. Rev. Mr. Rogers's society was

4

about to vacate the Odeon and occupy their new house on Winter Street. The Odeon could be obtained. The time, place, and circumstances, all seemed propitious. A council of pastors and influential laymen was convened, the subject was thoroughly discussêd, and the undertaking fully approved. North Russell Street Church, as elsewhere stated, contributed forty members of society. A less number came from Bennet Street Church, but there were more from the congregation. Isaac Rich and John Gove, especially desirable as financial pillars, were from that church. Only a few members came at first from Bromfield Street, but several influential families came at a later date. We cannot find the means of giving names and numbers from these churches, as we have done from Russell Street. It is proper to remark here that several influential persons, whom we shall have occasion to mention, came from churches out of the city, or united there as probationers. We think the whole membership, at the organization, was considerably less than one hundred.

A heavy pecuniary responsibility was cheerfully assumed by the new church, the rent alone being $1,500 per annum. Jacob Sleeper and John Borrowscale, of Bromfield and Church Street churches, agreed to aid in the payment of rent, if necessary. Beyond that no outside aid was expected.

John N. Maffitt was to supply the pulpit for a season, and as long as Providence seemed to indicate the propriety of his doing so. He had been preaching successfully in the city for several months to crowded houses.

The Odeon would accommodate, at least, 1,500 people. The preacher's popularity would fill the house, and the revival would continue under his labors. This was a rational anticipation. It is to be confessed that the expectation of a very large accession was not realized. The Society experienced some disappointments and trials.

Mr. Maffitt did fill the Odeon with an intelligent and interested congregation. But immediately he was elected Chaplain to the House of Representatives in Congress, and, comet-like, he was away. It had been well understood that his local attachments were not strong, but they had not reckoned on this emergency. They knew that some of his converts had the reputation of falling away, after a time; but it was known that a multitude of them adorned the Christian church, and that some of them were eminent and efficient ministers of the gospel. They supposed it only necessary to take good care of the converts, and all would be well. This the church was able and willing to do. The loss of Mr. Maffitt, at that time, was a serious drawback. The Society was variously supplied till the session of the New England Conference, when B. F. Tefft was stationed preacher in charge. His health broke down months before his year expired, and thereby came another affliction. Abel Stevens supplied the pulpit the remainder of the year; but, as he was editor of Zion's Herald, and resided out of town, he could not perform pastoral duties or attend the evening meetings. The preachers for the three years next succeeding, were Messrs. Miner Raymond, John T. Burrill, and Jefferson Hascall. We need not speak of the ability or zeal of any of these gentlemen. But the high expectations of the church were not met. The reason for this, however, is not attributable to any lack of service on the part of the pastors, or of religious energy on the part of the church. The cessation of the great revival throughout the city affected this as well as all the other churches in Boston, though to a less extent.

In 1846 the lease of the Odeon was surrendered, the church receiving some bonus; and the members of the church went, about one hundred of them to the Bromfield, and about fifty to the other churches.

To such as do not understand the whole matter, the undertaking seems to have resulted in a failure; but to the well-informed, and to the parties interested, it may and does seem a decided success.

What but a wish to promote the cause of Christianity could have induced wise men to advise this undertaking? It increased their own responsibilities in the several churches. What unworthy motive would incite the pioneers to assume a labor so arduous, or a responsibility so heavy? The salvation of souls, and the spread and honor of Methodism, were the motive power. And for these good intentions and noble sacrifices of those who went out to the battle, and of those who took care of the interests at home, there is an ample reward, unfailing, with Him whose glory was sought.

We have remarked that the church was disappointed in the number of conversions. This arose from having expected wonderful results. There were about 150 conversions during those four years; and we presume it was a better result, by far, than was realized by any other Methodist church in the city, during the same time. Lest there should seem a discrepancy in relation to numbers, it is important to state that many of the original members came, not like the leaders, with a fixed determination, but for no special purpose, and they left when it was for their interest or pleasure. So at the close of the term they had but little rising 150 members. Some of the converts had not been previous attendants of the Methodist church. Those who united with the church from probation were of a good class of people, desirable for their stability of character, and influence in the community. Many of them now sustain positions in the churches from which they could not well be spared. A few have gone triumphantly to the reward and home of the blest.

When this enterprise was commenced, it was among the designs of the parties interested to build a house of worship which would be more attractive to the young people of the church, and better adapted to public taste than any the Societies then had in the city. This was considered absolutely necessary to the prosperity of Methodism,— an opinion which has been fully justified by the purchase of the Hanover Street Church, by the renovation of the churches on Russell, Bromfield, and Church streets, and by the present building of the Tremont Avenue Church,— all of which has been accomplished since the commencement of 1846. When the time arrived for decision in relation to building, it was Christian-like to take a survey of the general interests of Methodism in Boston.

Some of the churches were much weaker than they had previously been. North Russell Street Church *must* be built, and there must be some foreign assistance for that purpose, consequently the Odeon people must expect less aid from the other churches than is usual on such occasions. However, the St. John's Church was thoroughly canvassed, and the result was encouraging and highly honorable. Additional subscriptions were promised from some of the other churches, and a satisfactory house of worship might have been erected, subject to incumbrances after the custom of the times. Still, considering the financial condition of the several churches, and the rather decreasing numbers in the membership, generally, building was of doubtful expediency. Perhaps the object of having a better house could be accomplished in another and better way.

A compact was made with the Bromfield Street Church, an account of which is inserted here, by request: —

" Records of a meeting of the two official boards of the Bromfield Street and St. John's churches, held on Saturday evening, May 16, 1846, at the Library Room of the Bromfield Street Church, to consider the propriety of uniting the said churches for the purpose of building a large and central Methodist house of worship in this city, whenever circumstances may be propitious.

" On motion, Rev. Charles Adams, of the Bromfield Street Church, was called to the chair; and D. S. King, of St. John's Church, was elected Secretary. The throne of grace was addressed by Rev. J. Hascall, of St. John's Church.

" After the object of the meeting had been stated, it was moved, That it is expedient for the Bromfield Street and St. John's churches to form a union, with a view of building a central church as soon as circumstances may render it proper. After a free interchange of views upon this subject, but without taking action upon the resolution, it being understood that the Bromfield Street board would hold a meeting on Monday evening next, it was voted to adjourn to Wednesday evening, May 20, at 7 o'clock, at the Bromfield Street vestry.

" D. S. King, *Secretary.*

" WEDNESDAY EVENING, MAY 20, 1846.

" The two official boards held a joint meeting pursuant to adjournment. Prayer by the Secretary. The minutes of the last meeting were read, and approved by vote.

" *Voted*, That the resolution before the meeting be laid upon the table for the purpose of hearing the Report of the Bromfield Street Board.

"After explanations by brother T. Patten, Thomas Bagnall, Jr., the Secretary, reported the proceedings of the Bromfield Street Board in relation to the proposed union.

" *Voted*, That the order of the day be taken up.

" The resolution of Saturday evening was carried without a dissenting vote.

" *Voted*, That the pastors of the two churches take measures to consummate this union at such time, and in such manner as they may deem proper.

" *Voted*, That all matters relating to building be referred to the Trustees.

" *Voted*, That we will use our best endeavors to make this contemplated union as strong as possible.

" *Voted*, That the Secretaries of the separate official boards be requested to copy the proceedings of this and the former meeting, into the books of records kept by the boards of Stewards and Leaders.

" The brethren present were Rev. C. Adams, Rev. J. Hascall, Messrs. Patten, Sleeper, Daggett, Pratt, Gale, Carr, Bagnall, Peirce, Snow, Parker, Nickerson, Motley, Wetherbee, Nutting, Flanders, G. W. King, Hinds, Tolman, Sinclair, Ewins, and the Secretary.

" The minutes of the present meeting were read and approved.

" *Voted* to adjourn *sine die*.   D. S. KING, *Secretary*."

With consent of the members, about one hundred, carrying nearly all the financial strength, became associated with the Bromfield Street Church. Those wishing to unite with other churches took their certificates. It should not be understood that the St. John's Church was given up of necessity. But for the agreement above recorded she would have pursued another course to carry out her original designs.

If any one supposes the church was weak, financially, or was deficient in persons capable of sustaining the spiritual interests of the Society, he will be undeceived by a knowledge of the membership. We give the names of some of the most prominent men in the Society, in alphabetical order. William C. Brown, Josiah A. Brodhead, Wm. Claflin, Francis E. Childs, Joseph R. Carr, Avery P. Ellis, John Gove, Milton Gale, Thomas Green, J. Wesley Griswold, George B. Gavitt, Charles E. C. Hadley, Cornelius Hamblin, W. T. Hannah, Anthony Holbrook, Truman R. Hawley, Joseph Hockey, Augustus Lothrop, Wm. W. Motley, Calvin S. Magoun, Thos. Montgomery, George A. Mansfield, Amos B. Merrill, W. D. Malcomb (now of the Vermont Annual Conference), Jacob S. Merrill, William Noble, Pliny Nickerson, Caleb Pratt, Caleb Pratt, Jr., Samuel F. Parker, Charles H. Peirce, Isaac Rich, George C. Rand, Thomas Restieaux, Robert Restieaux, Alvah Roundy, James S. Rutledge, Asa B. Snow, Isaiah Stoddard, Harvey Scudder, Alexander Wilson, Thomas Watson, Nahum Wetherbee. I might add the names of other very worthy men, who in quiet were more like the flower which blushes unseen, but the fragrance of whose memory will ever be precious to those who knew them best.

There was a band of Christian ladies, who for moral worth and religious enterprise were not a whit behind their husbands and friends. The prayer and class meetings were well attended, and well sustained. In this connection we will state that the facilities for meetings were good. The Society had the audience-room at pleasure Sabbath evenings, as well as in the day-time. The former saloon made a convenient and pleasant vestry for meetings during the week. The ladies had a flourishing benevolent society. The Sabbath School was one of the very best. Nearly all the principal personages were members of it. There was one Bible class of over sixty members, composed of those who were not needed as teachers.

The loss of such and so many members from the North

and West Ends was severely felt by those churches, when the day of adversity came upon them. It is true they have each received some aid for the purpose of building and purchase; but the amount was trifling compared with what the St. John men would have done, had they remained in the churches.

But it should be remembered that they might have left for other reasons, and some of them would have done so as a manifest destiny. And it should be still further considered that their absence gave a wider scope to the talent, energy, and labor of the members of these churches, and it is even probable that many made abler men and women, and better Christians, by having passed successfully through a crisis which demanded the exercise of their best energies, and an enlarged benevolence.

Bromfield Street Church, which could have done very well alone, was largely the gainer. Her contribution to the St. John's Church was restored many fold, in every respect. And what of it? She built a new house appropriate to the times; she was able to strengthen the weak in different places, and did it. And when the time came for a special effort, in a most important location, she was prepared to render essential financial aid, and a richer contribution from her membership, to the Tremont Avenue Church.

Personal results to the St. John members should not be overlooked. Comparatively they were young. They had not many of them ever borne very heavy burdens. They expected to do nobly. They were generous in all the collections of the church, for religious, charitable, and literary purposes. We recollect that the first year, they raised over seven dollars per member, missionary money. But their stability was put to a severe test. For reasons which we have stated the congregation was not more than one third as large as was expected. The current expenses were very high, and the members who could pay largely were few.

Sometimes the financial load appeared like an intolerable burden; but all hands, rich and poor, lifted with a will, and always successfully. We presume the members of the Official Board will not soon forget one of their darkest seasons, when a brother, whose later princely munificence has commanded admiration, walked the room demurely for a season, and then remarked, "I never say die." He subscribed $800, exclusive of pew-rent, toward the expenses of the year. We ought not to tell tales out of the Board, but this event is so much to our point that we cannot afford to lose it. All were inspired by the word and the deed. The financial work of that year was soon accomplished, and like efforts were repeated in succeeding years.

It was about these years that Boston Methodism made a rapid advance in her financial enterprise for the church. Better churches were required, preachers' salaries increased, missionary contributions enlarged, the Preachers' Aid Society better sustained, a Theological school established, and the Wesleyan University better endowed. And without any disrespect to the fathers, we may suggest that the more able members of the churches began to contribute more liberally, according to their means, than they had previously done.

The St. John brethren had their share of this improvement. And who can doubt that such a training is highly important to the development of a noble Christian character? There were other schools in Boston for such education, and apt scholars too. But the Odeon was an excellent institution of the kind; indeed, it might have ranked as a High School.

5

CHAPTER VII.

PASSING AWAY. — Jan. 22, 1861. Twenty-four years have come and gone. What changes have they brought. Our catalogue shows large accessions by certificate, and from probation. But of that long list, only 360 remain. We know of only twelve persons of the present congregation who were worshippers at the Wells School house, during the first six months. Three of them were children then. The visits of three of the number now are few and far between, but sometimes they come as good angels. Two of these are so infirm that they cannot be often present; the other resides out of town, but continues her membership here, and comes home occasionally as a fond mother to see her children.

Only about fifty have deceased while connected with this church. The others have been scattered far and wide. Many of them we know have gone to their rest; how many, the recording angel only can tell.

> " It is written on the skies
>   Of the soft blue summer day;
> It is traced in sunset's dies,
>   ' Passing away.'
>
> " It is written on the brow,
>   Where the spirit's ardent ray,
> Lives, burns, and triumphs now,
>   ' Passing away.' "   MRS. HEMANS.

As we search our records, and trace the history of the membership, "passing away" is most solemnly impressed upon our minds. We are passing away, but—

> " We know our fate is in his hands
> Whose wisdom guides the rolling year,
> Whose power upholds creation's plan,
> Whose mercy saves from dangers near;
> In his control,
> We leave our all;
> Safe in his love, why should we fear ? "
>
> FRANCES A. COLLINS.

MEMBERS DECEASED.—There have been but few aged members of the church. The great majority of those who have deceased were in the prime of life. The following named persons died at an advanced age.

Elizabeth Lakeman, aged 93 : she had been a member of the M. E. Church fifty years ; Nancy Copeland, aged 83 years, and Sarah Binney, a few years younger; they were sisters of Col. Amos Binney who was an early member of the first M. E. Church in Boston, and who in his day was, we suppose, the most wealthy and beneficent Methodist in New England.

Miss Binney was also an early member at "Methodist Alley." They were venerable Christian ladies, worthy of such a brother. Seth Lewis died in 1856. He was a good man, but much inclined to distrust himself. He had been many years an attendant at the Methodist Church, but united here on probation, and lived a peaceful Christian.

Ebenezer Thompson and wife removed their relation from this church before their decease. They were excellent Christian people, and were well known in New England. We think obituary notices of all these saints may be found in Zion's Herald.

Peninnah C. Robey died Oct. 20, 1838. This was the first death of a teacher in the Sabbath School. She was one of the original teachers, and was an excellent young lady. She died well.

A. H. Taylor died in 1858. He was an excellent teacher of a Bible class, and was a highly respected member of the Young Men's Christian Association.

MEMBERS FROM PROBATION. — We suppose about one half of the members of the church have been received from probation, though we have not denoted so many by the *star*. Sometimes the pastor has forgotten to record "how received." In consequence of this, some may appear to have been received by certificate who came from probation. The names of probationers who did not join the church in full connection, with the exception of a few who left by certificate, are not included in this catalogue. All those who are designated as present members, are in full connection. With due respect for all others, we may be allowed to say that the persons now living, who were received as probationers, would constitute a powerful church, if they could be brought together. We might readily suggest the names of those who have the wisdom to guide, the wealth to sustain, and the talent and piety to insure eminent success. The removal of many of the more prosperous of our members has been deeply regretted. At the same time there has been cause of profound gratitude that enough have remained to sustain the cause. While we would make no offensive distinctions, we must acknowledge the good providence which has kept the first two probationers with us all these years, and has blessed them with ample means and willing minds to be pillars of strength in every emergency.

WESLEYAN BENEVOLENT SOCIETY.—The ladies have had an efficient organization to aid the poor without regard to church membership. The Society has been generously sustained, and many a sad heart has been made glad through its instrumentality.

PASTOR'S BIBLE CLASS.—In 1838, Mr. Scudder had a Bible class of 35 members, which met on secular evenings. The great object of having this class was to prepare the teachers to do their work more efficiently. Since that time there have been Bible classes from which teachers might be selected. A Bible class in the Sabbath School, or rather in a separate room on the Sabbath, conducted by a competent teacher, might be of great advantage to the more advanced scholars in preparing them to teach. Genius and preparation are as necessary to success in the Sabbath, as in the common school.

CONVERSIONS OF SCHOLARS.—We find the report of fifty conversions in the school, in the Conference year closing in 1852. This is the highest number of any year; but such conversions have been numerous. Time has shown that they are valuable.

JUVENILE CLASS.—This department of the school was established June 23, 1839. Julia C. Hascall, pastor's wife, and Mary Ann Lewis, took the charge of it. Singing and oral instruction have been the principal work in this class. We judge that there may have been an average of fifty members of this class. It meets in a separate room, and is always a place of interest. Miss Lewis continued in this department about twenty-one years, and left it only on account of feeble health. Mary Mansfield and Nancy H. Newcomb have each had long terms of service in this department. Their principal work has been to teach the children in singing. Several other persons have been teachers for a short time. Miss Julia A. Wheaton succeeded Miss Lewis, but was obliged to desist to favor her voice. Miss Wheaton has devoted much time to singing and music for the benefit of the school. Mrs. Newcomb has laid the church under many obligations for services in the choir. Mrs. Susan Damrell, the present teacher of this class, and her husband, set the example of having parents and children attend Sabbath School together.

CONTINUANCE IN THE SABBATH SCHOOL.—John H. Collins has attended Sabbath School forty years, and still attends. He has been in this school nearly twenty years. Aside from the duties of Superintendent, his most prominent labor has been in preparing for the exhibitions. He has written many productions for these occasions, and has prepared several valedictories in verse. He may be considered the " Poet Laureate " of the school.

L. L. Tarbell has served as Superintendent considerably longer than any one else; and has been active in preparing for the anniversaries for many years.

Martha Cole, Harriet Sawyer, and Chas. H. Merritt, have each been teachers in the school more than twenty years.

Sarah E. Lewis was one of the original scholars. She entered the school as one of the *little* children. She has been a member ever since, with the exception of a few months, while employed as teacher in a mission school.

Wm. Blakemore and wife, with all their children, were regular attendants of the school, while connected with this Society.

VESTRY IMPROVED.—Late in 1859, the school obtained leave of the trustees to make some changes in the vestry. The old high-backed, stationary seats were removed; a new hard-pine floor was laid; the walls and ceilings were beautified; settees appropriate for the school and prayer meetings were procured; and all other necessary improvements made to render the vestry pleasant and convenient, at a cost of $500. The old seats were sold for $30; collections on this account amounting to $15 were made in the prayer meetings, and the balance, $465, was paid by the school. We place a high estimate on that operation.

A HISTORIAN.—It is recommended by high authority that the history of our churches and Sabbath Schools should be written, and the importance of having it done is generally admitted. It is an easy matter to devise such an undertaking, but quite another to get it accomplished. In preparing this small work, apparently a trifling job, we have had no small task. And having had some experience, we may be allowed a few suggestions, which may hereafter, if heeded, be of some advantage.

From our own experience, we apprehend that many of the records of churches and schools may be lost, and that those which have been preserved lack much of the material important to the interest of a history.

Under such circumstances it will be impossible for many of the earlier institutions to make out a full history. For the past they must do the best they can. But the past should suffice for such negligence, with us, at any rate.

We would *suggest* that there be a HISTORIAN for each church and Sabbath School, appointed to do all future work in season, whatever may become of the past. One person could readily keep the history of both the church and the school. We would not have the work of a historian pertain to the duties of any of our secretaries, but he should notice such events as they are not expected to record, and take from their records such abstracts as may be deemed proper.

If the work is neglected from year to year, the chances are that it will never be done. If done promptly, it will be accomplished with less expense, in less time, with more fulness, more accuracy, and more unction.

Titles.—It is from no lack of veneration, that we have omitted titles to a very great extent in this work. The Reverend clergy, Honorable gentlemen, and Esquires, will appreciate our motives in so doing.

A Last Word. — We have endeavored to write this history impartially, according to the principle laid down in the Preface. We have stated facts, but have not spoken in praise of the living. We hope the time will be long delayed when it will be proper to publish what it is in our heart to say of many persons who are, and of those who are not, named in this work.

No one is more fully aware than the editor, that this production might be improved by rewriting, but as our work is gratuitous, it would not pay, and the generous reader would not require it.

CHAPTER VIII.

OUR Sabbath School, as an organization, takes precedence of the church. It was instituted Jan. 22, 1837, the very day on which preaching was commenced in Blossom Street. The storm of that day, elsewhere noticed, was not sufficient to dampen the zeal of our pioneers. They met at noon, as per previous appointment, held religious exercises, appointed officers and committees, formed classes and selected teachers.

Most unfortunately and strangely, the Roll and Record books of our school, for the first twenty years, have been lost. We are consequently dependent on the memory and private memoranda of individuals, and on reports in which the school is but partially represented, for our data during that time. We have no list of the persons who organized the school, nor can we give a list of the officers and teachers. It is safe, however, to consider that nearly all the persons elsewhere mentioned as taking part in the formation of the new church, were connected with the school in some capacity. This is a matter of personal recollection. Albert H. Brown was elected Superintendent. Seven classes were formed.

Sarah Young, Mary Ann Lewis, Matilda Lewis, I. J. P. Collyer, and Thomas Patten, Jr., were appointed a committee to procure scholars. Members of the committee were active, and other parties aided them.

In twelve months the school numbered 28 teachers and 106 scholars. The religious interest of the school was not behind the zeal to add to its numbers. Previous to the Annual Conference of 1838, eleven scholars, mostly from the Bible classes, and eight teachers were reported to have been converted.

Albert H. Brown, Benj. H. Barnes, Joseph True, Sarah Jordan, and Phebe R. Young, were appointed a committee to .

procure a library. The library, however, was not procured for more than a year. Books were first given out from it, April 8, 1838. It then contained 300 volumes. This delay was not from any lack of enterprise on the part of the committee, but rather from a desire to promote the interest of the school, and the cause of Sabbath schools in general another way. Soon after our organization, the publication of the Sabbath School Messenger was proposed by a member of the school. ♦

Anxious to do what they could to secure the publication of such a periodical in the M. E. Church, the committee and the school thought it best to appropriate all their means to this object.

On the 12th of March they subscribed $20 to pay for fifty copies of the Messenger. They distributed the first No. (June) in the school on the 28th of May. The scholars were very well supplied with books from the private libraries of the teachers, during that year.

We have been furnished with a few items which will indicate the zest with which our teachers commenced their work. Waiving extreme delicacy, we give them as they were received. Feb. 26, 1837, the school had a public monthly examination. March 12, a public address was delivered before the school by D. S. King. April 6, the school held its first annual exhibition. April 16, the teachers held their first prayer meeting. April 22, 1838, D. S. King and Ezra Mudge were appointed a committee to visit other schools. These appointments were pursuant to mutual arrangement with all the Methodist schools in the city. Each school appointed two delegates. The body of delegates had their arrangements so that all the schools should be visited systematically.

This at the time was considered very beneficial. The delegates generally spent a little time in addressing the schools for their edification and encouragement, and at the same time they had the advantage of observation, which would enable them to suggest improvements at home. This plan had been in operation the year before, and it was while in pursuit of such duties that the publication of the Messenger was resolved upon by the publisher. We have thus narrated the principal events of the first year, up to the Annual Conference of 1838, to give some idea of our commencement, but we design to present the rest of our history in chapters classified according to the nature of the subject, rather than as annals, as that is more convenient, and we think will be more interesting.

CHAPTER IX.

It has been a point well understood in this school, that however able the teachers may be to impart instruction, the interest of the children is heightened by a change and variety of exercises. The teachers have not been slow to devise measures in the school and out of it, calculated to make the children happier and wiser than they would be under a rigid routine of instruction, and to attach them to the school.

This school, like all others, has been opened with singing, reading the Scriptures, and prayer. The Scriptures have been read by the Superintendent and the school, a verse alternately; the teachers and children reading in concert. This reading sounds pleasantly, and enlivens the children, in addition to improvement in reading and the benefit of the lesson. After the extemporaneous prayer, the Lord's Prayer has been repeated in concert, and we think very profitably. Besides the usual opening and closing exercises, and attention to the lessons, we will mention several matters which have been of interest to the children.

New scholars are admitted, and retiring ones discharged, by vote of the school. This is made a matter of importance, and the children attend to it as an affair in which they have a personal responsibility.

The school has been frequently addressed by pastors, teachers, official and other visitors. The official visits have been discontinued since the dissolution of the union, elsewhere mentioned, but their place has been supplied to a great extent by other guests, many of whose addresses have been of thrilling interest.

At an early date we commenced preaching to the children. In the great revival of 1840-1, it became a matter of necessity to keep them in the vestry, afternoons, as there was no place for them in the audience-room. The services were adapted to their capacity. We had singing, prayer, sermons prepared for them, or "Todd's Lectures to Children." The practice of preaching to them occasionally, has been continued by our preachers. On such occasions they have generally been seated together in the central pews. They richly enjoy such a treat, and the delight of the adult part of the congregation is not diminished.

The monthly or quarterly examinations have served a good purpose. They prevented a sameness of exercises, improved the talent for declamation, and called together parents and friends not accustomed to attend the school, and delighted all with many precious lessons from poets and orators.

The annual excursion to some delightful grove is always a source of high anticipation, is promotive of health and sociability, and has sometimes been the means of additions to the school.

Books from our excellent library have been of immense advantage to many of the children, while Sabbath School papers have performed their mission of love successfully. The " Sabbath School Messenger" and " Advocate " have been hailed with delight among us, and now the " Teachers' Advocate " comes also, a welcome and interesting guest.

Social Interviews of teachers and scholars have strengthened the bond of union, while the " Social Monitor," prepared by the school and read at these assemblies, has elicited the talent of the teachers and amused the children; so genius and sociability have been happily combined.

The anniversaries have been occasions of deep interest to teachers, scholars, and friends. They have been gotten up with great labor, care, and skill. Sometimes the entire matter for our exhibition has been prepared expressly for the occasion, and without going out of the congregation for assistance. Aside from the improvement of talent by teachers and scholars, and a specially good time, an admission fee to the extent of a crowded house has been cheerfully paid, thus making an agreeable source of revenue for the benefit of the school.

The Monthly Concert of prayer in behalf of Sabbath Schools has been held generally, and well sustained. The services on these occasions have been varied according to the circumstances of the school and the church.

They have commenced with several "short prayers," interspersed with singing; after which for a season the children have recited proof-texts, or answered questions proposed by the Pastor or Superintendent. At other times addresses have been made pertinent to the Sabbath-School cause, or to the instruction and conversion of the children. It has, however, always been understood that strict conformity to the expressed object of the meeting was not required. Making this allowance, there has been much freedom of speech and spirit in the meetings. Strangers have sought the benefit of them; the interest of our own people has been enlivened, and the children who attended, have been delighted, and some of them have been converted. In times of deep religious interest, penitents have been called to the altar at the close of the meeting. This "monthly concert" with us has answered the design of the originators. Sometimes in seasons of deep religious interest, the services of the regular session of the school have been changed to a prayer meeting, with very happy results.

The weekly missionary collections have been interesting to the children. The hour has passed the more pleasantly for them; they have been trained to a regular system of benevolence, and the amount raised has been of importance to the cause.

The children have generally been desirous of contributing to the cause. The excitement of putting the money in the box has perhaps been a small consideration with the little ones, and emulation has done its work, but we think that Christian principle has been at the foundation. They love the heathen, and desire to do them good.

When our school was in its infancy, the establishment of foreign missions by the M. E. Church had just commenced, and it was necessary to make increased exertions. Various measures were adopted. The children in this school appropriated money to educate children in Oregon and Africa with Christian names, which they delighted to honor. The money came freely for such a purpose. We have no doubt it was spent with economy and to the best advantage. Usually and most properly the funds have been raised for general purposes.

In November, 1837, when D. P. Kidder and R. McMundy were about to embark on their mission to Rio Janeiro, they held a meeting with the children of our schools at the Bennet Street Church. The children became enthusiastic, and many of them took a pledge to deny themselves of tea, coffee, and sugar for one year, provided their parents would give them one cent a day for the missionary cause. We are unable to say how many parents consented, or how many of the children kept the pledge. We know that some were true to their agreement. Of such was Albert, the son of our Superintendent. But his zeal was not bounded by $3.65. After trying this self-denial one day and finding it easy, he contemplated a larger operation. So he said, "Father, what do you suppose I have been thinking about?" "I do not know, my son; what is it?" I have been thinking about going without butter; will you give me ten dollars a year if I will go without butter?" "Ten dollars, my son, is a very large sum of money." "Well, the missionaries want a good deal of money to buy so many books (Bibles), and you know I love butter very much, and a year is a great while, and I ought to have a large sum." These were arguments which the father could not resist. The bargain was concluded, and kept by both parties. His friends made up the amount to $14, by deposit in his missionary box. Two very small brothers, members of our school, resolved to do something entirely upon their own resources. They picked up in the street 1,300 peach-stones, cracked them and sold the meat for thirteen cents, and paid over the money. At a little later date, Charlie Woodbury, when six years of age, denied himself of butter for six cents a week to raise money for his favorite missionary cause.

Missionary boxes were common in the families, and the deposits were brought to the Sabbath School.

Sometimes we read letters in the school which were sent to the editor of the Messenger for publication. Some of these appeals were excellent. Franklin Haven of Malden, a sick little boy who died a few months afterwards, sent $1.50 for the cause, with an appeal to children. Harriet Binney, now Mrs. Daniel Steele, addressed the "Young Sisters," and at the same time forwarded $2 for missions, $1 from her missionary box, and $1 of her own earnings. We insert Franklin's letter.

My Young Friends: For three years past I have been sick, and am not able to help myself. Yet I do not murmur; I feel that God does right. I do not expect to live long; but I am willing to die, for I feel that I shall go to heaven and be happy.

I have thought a great deal lately about the poor heathen, and though I am a sick boy, yet I am better off than they; for I have the Bible, and can pray and think about heaven. I have thought, too, that we children can do something to help them. I have been saving a little money, and have sent it to the editor of the Messenger for the missionary cause. We can all do a little, — let us try.　　FRANKLIN HAVEN.

MALDEN CENTRE, FEB. 26, 1838.

CHAPTER X

It has been the great object of this school to instruct the children in all the lessons of Holy Writ, to lead their souls to the fountain of love, and to educate them to *do* the will of the Lord. One subject, we think, has received unusual attention. In the Sabbath School, at the Sabbath-school Concert, and the Missionary prayer meeting, the importance of education as one qualification for usefulness in any sphere of life, and especially in the work of the holy ministry, should any be called to that, has been frequently and powerfully urged. This has not been without good effect upon the children, and the young teachers in the school, in directing their course of education, or upon the older teachers in their efforts in behalf of others.

The consistent teacher, who prays the Master to send more laborers into the vineyard, will do all in his power to qualify those under his charge, by the cultivation of talent, education, and grace, for a glorious work in the harvest of souls. Keen eyes have watched with interest the development of character among our young people, and when the genius and virtues of any have seemed to designate them as fit subjects for a " holy calling," they have been advised, encouraged, and aided, if necessary, in the acquirement of an education. Here follows a list of the persons who have entered the regular work of the ministry, and who were once connected with this charge in the church or Sabbath School. All were members of the church, excepting Mr. Brown and Mr. True. They were quite young when members of the school.

I. J. P. Collyer, of the New England Conference, teacher.

Daniel Wise, Providence Conference. He improved every opportunity to labor in the school, but could not be regular.

Being a local preacher his services were in much demand elsewhere. His principal labor in the school was by way of addresses and sermons to the children.

Edward A. Lyon, of Providence Conference, teacher.

Amos P. Battey, of Maine Conference, teacher.

Charles W. Kellogg, Vermont Conference, teacher.

Joshua B. Holman, New Hampshire Conference, teacher and superintendent.

George Dunbar, New York East Conference, teacher.

Sullivan Holman, New Hampshire Conference, teacher.

Charles A. G. Brigham, pastor of the Presbyterian Church, Enfield, Connecticut, scholar and officer.

Calvin Holman, New Hampshire Conference, teacher.

Wm. S. Studley, New York East Conference, scholar, teacher, superintendent, and pastor.

Jonas M. Bailey, New England Conference, teacher.

Albert H. Brown, Jr., Newark Conference, scholar.

Edward Hyde True, Rector of St. Stephen's Church, Lynn (Protestant Episcopal) scholar.

Ichabod Marcy, New England Conference, belonged to the church in 1841, but could not attend the Sabbath School. In fact, his connection with the church was mainly for the purpose of a recommendation to the Annual Conference; so as we can claim no particular credit on his account, we will cherish a remembrance of his name as a compliment to us, and a token that he is not forgotten.

Messrs. Marcy, Brigham, Studley, Bailey, Brown, and True, all graduated at the Wesleyan University, Middletown, Conn. Nearly all the others have been hard students at an Academy or Theological School. In the exception there is proof that men can be self-made, and that a liberal education, however desirable, is not absolutely requisite to popularity and success. Three of the number were called to the work of the ministry after they had assumed the cares of a family.

Henry Morgan, in charge of the Boston Union Mission, was a member of the church in 1851, but his duties did not permit him to labor in the school. Mr. Morgan is a local preacher.

Wm. H. Woodbury, the author of several popular German school-books, was a local preacher with us, but his Sabbath services were so much in requisition that his appearance in the school was but occasional. When he did come, his influence was beneficial. We have forgotten his Alma Mater. After leaving us he studied two or three years in Germany.

George L. Roberts, who had the valedictory at the Wesleyan University in 1859, was brought up in our school till he had for a considerable time been known as the youngest member of the church, and until he left the city to acquire an education. The members of our school were so much gratified with his success that they caused a certificate of Life Membership in the Sabbath School Union of the Methodist Episcopal Church, to be presented to him, Commencement Day, by Prof. True, a former pastor. George said he hardly knew whether he was the more pleased with the certificate or his parchment.

Charles A. Stowell, one of the original scholars, graduated at Williams College.

W. H. W. Hinds, assistant physician at the Almshouse, in Amesbury, was for several years a member of our school.

Five of our former scholars are now in college.

John L. S., son of Reuben Roberts, Charles Olin, son of Elijah Brigham, John Clark, son of Franklin Rand, and Charles True, son of Samuel Adams, are all at the Wesleyan University. Nelson S. Cobleigh is a member of McKendree College. Wm. North Rice, son of a former pastor, was a member of the juvenile class. He has been fitted for college some time, and expects to enter at a suitable age.

Many of our scholars, male and female, have acquired a competent education for the business or accomplishments of life in our excellent public and private city schools; but it does not come within the purview of this work to speak of them. We deem it proper, however, to make some mention of the ladies who have shared in the work of the Itinerancy, or been employed as teachers, and have acquired their position *after* having been in the school. Miss Hannah M. Thompson, teacher, became Preceptress of Wilbraham Academy, and afterwards the wife of Rev. Dr. Humphrey Pickard.

Matilda Lewis, teacher, is the wife of I. J. P. Collyer, of the New England Conference.

Elizabeth Thornton, teacher, is the wife of Benjamin Lufkin, of the East Maine Conference.

Elizabeth Moore is the wife of H. P. Andrews, of the New England Conference.

Frances A. Collins, teacher, was several years a teacher in the Wells School. She became the wife of Wm. S. Studley, now of New York East Conference.

Sarah L. Holman, teacher, is the wife of J. B. Holman, of the New Hampshire Conference.

Of the young ladies who have grown up from childhood in our school, and belonging to permanent families in the church, Mrs. Maria E. Tucker has been, and Sarah E. Lewis, Adeline S. and Frances M. Bodge, Julia A. Wheaton, and Helen W. Avery, now are teachers in our public schools. As three of these ladies are upon our committee, it is important to state that this particular item has not been submitted to them.

We have spoken of the causes which have given some impetus to the educational interest among our young people.

The literary acquirements of many whose names appear in this history are well understood. We ought to acknowledge the salutary influence of others, whose names would otherwise be found only in the catalogue. Amos B. Merrill, from the Wesleyan University, was the teacher of an interesting Bible class, while a student at the Harvard Law School.

Joseph True, one of the original teachers, was at the time a law student. He died many years ago. We have no sufficient data for an obituary notice.

Dr. E. O. Phinney, graduate of the Wesleyan University, was a teacher.

Joseph W. Cushing, graduate of the Wesleyan University, and a house surgeon at the McLean Hospital, is a present member of the school.

One point is, that, superadded to good teaching and interesting addresses, the presence of literary persons is a living suggestion to the children upon the subject of education.

Making all due allowance for the fact that some came only to bless us, and that some have belonged to other schools as well as to ours, we still have very gratifying results in the number and character of those who have entered the ministry, and of those who have acquired or are in pursuit of an education adequate to the more public stations in life. When we review our list of pastors, and recollect the many eminent and faithful teachers who have been in the school, we cannot consider the result a mere matter of course. It is the fruit of more than ordinary genius, qualification, toil, and prayer.

To Him be the praise and the glory, now and forever. Amen.

CHAPTER XI.

THE Messenger was "brought out" and introduced to the public as an interesting young lady. She was dressed in green; the jewels of her coronet were, "Her ways are ways of pleasantness, and all her paths are peace." And on her breast-plate was a vignette with a lady, pointing youth and children to a cross, around which were beams of light. Her personal beauty and decorations, however, were not her chief attraction.

It was her brilliant talent, her sublime moral character and deep-toned piety, which commanded admiration. Wherever she went, she was received as a favorite guest.

But, like most other misses, she early formed an alliance which involved a change of name. Although the groom was more than three years her junior, she followed conventional usage, and assumed the name of her partner. This was the less to be regretted as that name was one of high distinction. She "still lives" in a neighboring city, and pays us frequent visits. It is our purpose to give some account of her early history.

Without any figure of speech, we think the first Sabbath School periodical published in the church, deserves a history; and we know of no more appropriate place for it, than in connection with the school to which its originator belonged.

The first number of the Sabbath School Messenger appeared for June, 1837. It was in pamphlet form, 24 pages to a monthly number, a volume making 288 good-sized pages, set in type conveniently large for young eyes, and making a generous amount of reading. The cover was as above suggested. It contained some pictorial illustrations, but not many.

The price was 50 cents per copy, or twenty dollars for fifty copies sent to one address.

The list of subscribers the first year amounted to about 3,000. The two churches in Lowell took 216 copies; Bromfield St. 86 ; Church St., 60 ; Charlestown, 60 ; Great Falls, 59 ; Lynn Common, 56; Nashua, 54 ; Marlboro', 53 ; Dover, Holliston, Ipswich, Manchester Mills, Conn., Portland, Chestnut St., in Providence, and Blossom St., Boston, 50 each. Some others of the more flourishing schools took from 10 to 30 copies, but much the larger number were sent to single subscribers, scattered far and wide. They went as far west as Green Bay, Wis. Ter., and to the South. One church in Louisville, Ky., took 33 copies. The chief patronage, however, was in New England.

The Messenger was edited and published the first two years by Dexter S. King. At the close of this time, it was changed to newspaper form. The principal reasons for doing this, were to avoid the expense of covers and of stitching, and thereby being able to present more reading for the same money, and to reduce the postage. At that time the postage on a small pamphlet was two cents, most absurdly, while on a large newspaper it was only one cent. The three years next succeeding, it was edited and published by Daniel Wise. During a part of this time, Mr. Wise had some connection with E. A. Rice, of Lowell, in the publishing department. The sixth volume was published by D. S. King, and edited by Edward Otheman, who also edited the seventh volume, for the new publisher. George C. Rand became the proprietor and publisher in 1843, and remained so till he sold out to the Methodist Book Concern in 1846. Bradford K. Peirce was editor the last two years.

The Sabbath School Advocate, established late in 1840, had become a prosperous paper. The Book Agents wanted the whole field for the Advocate, but they did not wish to enter into competition with the Messenger in New England. They proposed to buy the Messenger list. It was hard to part with so dear a friend, but Mr. Rand and others thought that on the whole it would be best. So the Messenger was merged in the Advocate.

There was always a kind regard for the Messenger on the part of church officials at New York. At a conference in Western New York, Bishop Hedding, Dr. Bangs, and one of the Book Agents spoke a kind word for it in open conference. They may have done the same in other places.

The circulation of the Messenger increased from year to year, so that at the time of its transfer it had over 20,000 subscribers.

We wish to claim for the Messenger a good reputation for literary ability and deep-toned piety. And we do so with a personal disclaimer, however, on the part of the first editor. And how could it be otherwise? Not to mention many excellent friends, pastors, and teachers, who contributed more or less, we will name some of our principal correspondents: Daniel Wise, Edward Otheman, Abel Stevens, Charles K. True, Joshua W. Downing, James Mudge, Jr., Bradford K. Pierce, Dr. Wm. A. Alcott, B. F. Nutting, Moses L. Scudder, Amos Binney, Mrs. Prof. Holdich, Marguerite O. Stevens, Priscilla P. Morse, Bethiah G. Haven, Hannah M. Thompson, Mrs. Sigourney, and Mrs. Maxwell. We will stop here, but not for want of honored names. All these wrote for the Messenger for the sake of making it interesting. It is well known that they could supply matter for periodicals, to delight children or princes at their pleasure.

It is an interesting fact that Mr. Rand, then quite a young man, commenced business in one room, with the Messenger as a nucleus. He has never moved his location, but has extended his premises immensely. His present establishment (Geo. C. Rand & Avery) is not excelled in magnitude or in the excellence of mechanical execution by any printing house in New England. This is a wonderful tree from such an acorn and in time so brief; but we must attribute its growth to the skill of the forester.

Another incident which may be amusing to some persons is, that Mr. Wise when a young man, became known as a writer through the Messenger. Who can say, that but for the opportunity thus offered, the genius of his pen might not have been otherwise employed. However that might have been, one thing is certain, the man who walks the quarter deck of our great Sunday School ship, was with us before the mast. He was a good hand then; is a good captain now. Success to him.

While he holds his present position we may feel assured that the lady introduced at the commencement of this chapter will retain her vigor and grace.

CHAPTER XII.

As Sabbath School conventions, denominational and union, for districts, associations, and the State, have become prevalent in this country, it is due to the claims of history that their origin should be kept in remembrance. We know of nothing of the kind in New England previous to their commencement by the M. E. Church in Boston District, and we are sure there had been no systematic plan for meetings of this description.

In the autumn of 1837, the editor of the Sabbath School Messenger proposed to B. Otheman, Presiding Elder of Boston District, the holding of such a convention. The suggestion met his approbation. He called a meeting of ministers and laymen in Boston, to consider the question. The object met with unanimous approval. Pursuant to order, a committee issued the call for a convention, too lengthy for insertion here, but as it was our first we make an extract.

" We could say much respecting the importance of such a convention, and present many considerations as inducements for a general attendance; but we cannot believe that you need much argument on this subject; you have long felt that something must be done to operate as a stimulus to the glorious cause of Sunday Schools among us, which, in too many instances, is in a languishing state, just breathing the breath of life. You are aware, that not only is something wanted to give such schools a healthy and vigorous tone, but also to encourage and hold up the hands of Sabbath School teachers in general; many of whom, to their praise be it spoken, have for years, through the summer's heat, and winter's cold, through storm and sunshine, been engaged in their humble, noiseless, and in many respects thankless employment; an

8

employment, however, that is conferring upon the world the highest possible benefit.

"Such a convention as we have now in view, is, we believe, a desideratum. The superintendents and teachers coming together as they will from various places, expressing to each other their views on Sabbath School instruction, and the best mode of conducting such instruction, — illustrating their remarks, perhaps, by facts which come under their own observation, — cannot fail to render the occasion one of thrilling interest. And who can conceive what will be the glorious results? — results which will have a life when we shall be sleeping in the dust, — when we shall be assembled at the judgment-seat, and when we shall be forever with the Lord.

"The sacrifice of time and money which our attendance upon the Convention may cost, though considerable, especially in these hard times, will, we trust, be more than balanced in your estimation by the magnitude of the object proposed.

"Your affectionate brethren in Christ,

D. S. KING,   J. SLEEPER,   ⎱
J. HORTON,   A. H. BROWN, ⎬ *Committee.*"
B. OTHEMAN,   ⎰

The Convention was held at the Bromfield Street Church, Boston on the 15th, 16th, and 17th of November. The District was well and ably represented from its different parts.

"It was organized with the following officers. HON. SETH SPRAGUE, JR., *President;* REV. TIMOTHY MERRITT, REV. B. OTHEMAN, MR. JONA. TUTTLE, and HON. EZRA MUDGE, *Vice Presidents;* REV. EDWARD OTHEMAN and MR. B. F. NUTTING, *Secretaries;* D. S. KING, *Corresponding Secretary.*" We have no list of the delegates present. Those from our school were A. H. Brown, D. S. King, B. H. Barnes, Joseph True, Thomas Patten, Jr., Mary Ann Lewis, Phebe R. Young, Sarah Jordan, and Matilda Lewis. A long series of resolutions, pertaining to the ways and means by which pastors, superintendents, and teachers might make their labors more effective, were discussed and adopted. One measure entirely new was recommended, as follows : —

"*Resolved*, That a Monthly Concert of prayer in behalf of the cause of Sabbath Schools, be held on the third Sabbath evening of every month, wherever practicable."

" It was also; *Resolved*, That it is expedient to hold a Convention on this District, similar to the present, once a year."

The report of the doings of the Convention was made by a committee composed of Jacob Sleeper, E. Otheman, and B. F. Nutting. They say : " In the course of the sittings of the Convention, they attended a public exhibition of the Methodist Sabbath Schools of the city. The delivery of a most timely and interesting discourse by the Presiding Elder of the District, on the qualifications, difficulties, and encouragements of the Sabbath School teacher, and a public meeting where most profitable and interesting addresses were made by the President of the Convention, and Rev. Messrs. Howard, Stevens, and Scudder." In closing the report, the committee express the opinion that this Convention " will have a very decided influence in favor of the Sabbath School cause."

The Convention was held the next year at the Common Church in Lynn. It was largely attended, and here for the first time a Sabbath School love feast was held among us. E. Otheman, the Secretary, reports that it was a " deeply interesting occasion, and formed a very appropriate closing exercise to a very harmonious, profitable, and delightful meeting for the improvement of Sabbath Schools."

Thus were Sabbath School conventions introduced in this vicinity, and they have been continued by the Methodists to the present time, and have become common in other denominations.

CHAPTER XIII.

DEAR BRETHREN AND FRIENDS : —

In answer to your call for information respecting my former connection with the North Russell Street Church and Sabbath School, perhaps I cannot do better than to send you the following extract from my introductory discourse as pastor of that church in the Spring of 1856 : —

"The holiest memories of my life not only cluster about Boston, as the place of my birth and the home of my childhood, but about this particular section of the city. Almost my entire history, for the first twenty-five years of my life, lingers about this spot. I was born on Russell Street, within a very short distance of the place where I now stand. The first school that I ever attended was on Russell Street, directly opposite my father's house. I passed nearly all the days of my boyhood right here. It was along these streets that I trundled my hoop. It was down these hills that I coursed my sled. It was in this sky that I flew my kite. It was just here that I engaged in the various merry sports of childhood ; — so that I almost know and love the very stones which pave the streets around us.

"And not only the personal history of my boyhood, but more especially my early religious experience, dates back to this very spot. This church was my nursing-mother in Christ. She took me in her arms, when I was spiritually distressed and helpless, and bore me to the cross of Calvary for strength and succor. She offered many fervent and effectual prayers in my behalf. She rejoiced with me in the day of my justification by faith in Christ. She shielded me, again and again, in seasons of severe spiritual conflict. She wept with me in the day of my deepest sorrow. She encouraged me in the way of usefulness, when I was struggling for an education. She bore with my weakness when I scarcely had a claim upon her affection ; and now, in return for her early love and forbearance, I come back to her and pour into her bosom my affectionate remembrances and thanks.

"My relation to this church has been very peculiar. There may be those here present, who remember the morning of Saturday, March 19, 1842, when I came, before sunrise, into the little vestry of the former chapel, and as a person seeking pardon and peace, requested the pastor, Rev. C. K. True, and the brethren present with him, to remember me in their prayers. Some of you may remember that beautiful Spring morning. I can never forget it. It was the beginning of better days with me. The day before, while engaged about my customary occupation, I had formed the purpose, deliberately and devoutly, that, if it were possible, I would be a Christian. It was the execution of this purpose which brought me here in search of prayer and counsel.

"On the Sunday next . but one following,—the 27th of March,—I joined Father Ezra Mudge's Bible-class, and remained a member of it only one or two Sundays, when I was placed in charge of a Bible-class myself. Not long afterwards I was elected to the office of Assistant Superintendent of the Sabbath School, in which office I continued about a year, when I was elected Superintendent, and served in that capacity till I left the city, in the summer of 1844, to enter upon my collegiate preparatory studies.

"But my relation to this church has been more peculiar, and more full of incident, than my Sabbath-School relation. It was here that I first joined a class ; that class was brother Benjamin Welch's. It was here that I was received into the church, when my term of probation had expired. It was at this altar that I first partook of the sacrament of the Lord's Supper. It was by the Quarterly Conference of this church that I was licensed to preach the gospel. It was here that I first met with her whom so many of you knew and loved, and whose gentle spirit lingers about our hearts to-day,— her who for years was the angel that encouraged my endeavors to be useful. We were married at this altar, and it was from this sacred spot, fifteen months afterwards, that I carried her out to her last resting-place. As I stand upon this spot, hallowed by so many sacred associations, I can almost hear that voice which said to Moses, 'Put off thy shoes from off thy feet, for the place whereon thou standest is holy ground.'

"And now, in accordance with your expressed wish to the authorities of the church, I have come to be your pastor. I need not say that I am happy to enter upon this relation among you; but as I look around upon this congregation, my joy is tinged with sadness, because I miss so many of the old familiar faces that used to be seen here. Where are the aged pilgrims that used to journey this way towards Mount Zion? Father Childs, that man of prayer and faith;—Father Mudge, whose face shone among us here, like the face of Moses among the children of Israel;—Father Lewis, that quiet, retiring, unobtrusive disciple of the Lord Jesus Christ;—these fathers,—where are they? Their journey is ended. They have passed the river. They have entered the pearly gates. They tread the golden pavement. They sing the new song. We, their children and fellow-disciples, follow after, trusting in the same God and Saviour.

"To me, this is indeed a sacred spot. In view of what she has done for me, I can say of this church, as the exiled prophet said of Jerusalem: 'If I forget thee, let my right hand forget her cunning; if I do not remember thee, let my tongue cleave to the roof of my mouth.'"

CHAPTER XIV

REV. J. AUGUSTUS ADAMS. — Died of consumption in San Francisco, California, August 27, 1860, Rev. John Augustus Adams, of the New England Conference, aged 42 years. He was born in South Newmarket, N. H., March 17, 1818, and was the son of Rev. J. F. Adams, of the New Hampshire Conference. He disclosed no marked religious feelings or purposes during his childhood and youth. He fitted for college at Newbury, Vt., and graduated from the Wesleyan University in 1842. He made a public profession of religion while in college in 1840, and was united in marriage to Miss Sophia M. Metcalf, of Greenland, N. H., Sept. 4, 1842. He spent two years as principal of an academy in Norwich, Conn., and one year at the Theological School in Andover. When the New Hampshire Conference Seminary was opened, he and his companion were employed as its first teachers.

He was admitted to the New England Conference in 1846, and was stationed at Medford, afterwards at Walpole, Watertown, two years, Lynn, Common Street, two years, Saugus, Russell Street, Boston, two years, Walpole as supernumerary, Salem and Melrose two years. Towards the close of the second year in Melrose, he was obliged to desist from ministerial labor on account of declining health.

Bro. Adams was a modest and unassuming man. He loved quiet and retirement, was cheerful and happy at home and in the society of chosen and congenial friends, but mingled little in general society, except for the performance of duty. He possessed a lively, vigorous, and cultivated mind, an inventive, mechanical genius, and a refined taste. He was very active and diligent, rose early, was methodical in his mode of life, and was characterized by gravity, dignity, and gentlemanly manners.

As a Christian, he was very devout, sincere, conscientious, and remarkably firm in his purposes. He was irreproachable in life, faithful in duties, and incorruptible in his integrity. He was kind-hearted, hospitable, and unselfish. His Christian character was marked by well-established principles, rather than by lively emotions. As a Christian minister, he was sincere, faithful, and instructive. He sought out acceptable words, prepared his sermons with great care, and illustrated the truth fully, pertinently, and forcibly. His delivery was lively and earnest; he varied his themes so as to interest and profit his hearers, giving to all a portion in due season, and often urged with great force and pungency the claims of Christ, and the great moral principles that are enjoined by the law of God. His ministry was fruitful, particularly in Lynn, Watertown, and Melrose. Gracious revivals attended his labors, and many in these and other places will remember him as the instrument of their conversion and spiritual advancement. He anxiously followed penitents to their homes, and privately and affectionately strove to show the heavenly way. He filled important stations honorably to himself and profitably to the church.

On account of still declining health, physicians advised him to seek a milder climate, and he therefore sailed for California 5th of February, 1860. He failed to realize the object he sought in that distant land. He suffered extremely in his voyage out; he travelled, lived in the mountains, used medical treatment, but finally was obliged to yield to the power of death. In the prime of his manhood he has fallen. Kindred, friends, and the church mourn his loss.

To his brother and his wife he wrote, August 23 : "I have found the end of my travels. Here in this beautiful Eldorado I think the Saviour indicates that he shall call me away to my final rest. To his holy will I give up my will. I am a firm believer in immortality ; I expect to share in the blessings of eternal life through faith in Christ. My longing desire is that you both secure the love of Jesus and a place in his kingdom."

The day before he died, too weak to write, he dictated a letter, in which, after asking the loving forgiveness of wife, parent, brother, and sister, for any wrong or grief he might ever have caused, he says: "I have no plea to make but that the blood of Jesus Christ cleanseth from all sin. Jesus Christ by the grace of God tasted death for every man. I trust these and all such promises by faith in Jesus Christ. He has promised to save all those that put their trust in Christ. As I lie here, so utterly weak, I can do this, and this is all I can do; I pray God to save my soul in his kingdom, and to meet you all there."

The day that he died, when told he could not live forty-eight hours, he whispered, with emphasis, "Glory to God, glory to God." Mrs. Gay, who, with her sister, Miss Smith, ministered to him with the tenderest affection and assiduity, says: "He died without the least struggle; it did not seem like dying; it seemed only like going to sleep."

"He sleeps in Jesus; lessed sleep,
From which none ever wake to weep."

OF A PAST SUPERINTENDENT.

Hon. Ezra Mudge. — Ezra Mudge was born in the year 1780, in the town of Lynn, Mass. We claim for him no uncommon birth, or gifts of genius above his fellows. And yet he was a remarkable man. Born amidst the scenes and excitement of the Revolution, he early imbibed the spirit and breathed the air of patriotism. Added to this, and still more important in the formation of his character, when but yet a lad, he became a convert to the then unpopular doctrines of Methodism, just introduced into New England, and from principle united with that feeble band of despised and persecuted people. We consider early piety as eminently conducive to the formation and development of Christian character. This youthful Christian enjoyed the benefit of rigid industry to aid his physical development, of strict temperance to promote his health and strengthen his intellect, and ample opposition to his religious faith and practice to guard him against the allurements of the world, and in an uncommon degree, the sympathy and love of his chosen associates to cheer him in the way of faith. Thus he became early established as a Christian; deeply rooted and grounded in love, and firmly fixed in principle, experience, and practice, as a disciple of Jesus.

Endowed by nature with good abilities, and aided by these advantages, he was early and thoroughly prepared for the duties of life, as a citizen and a Christian. While quite a young man, he added to the cares of a family and of business occupation, strict attention to the interests of the church, and was ever ready to stand in his place, as a citizen and a patriot.

In 1807 he was elected representative to the Legislature of Massachusetts; and for sixteen years he served his native town in that capacity. These years included the time of our last war with England. Living exposed upon the sea coast, the homes and lives of his people were in danger. His courage was put to the test. He was active in the formation of an artillery company, and in 1813 the gentle Ezra Mudge was commissioned as its captain, — an office then of danger and responsibility. But we cannot doubt that in case of the anticipated emergency, his bravery would have been commensurate with his position, and he could have shouted like the ancient leader of Israel: "Blessed be the Lord, my strength, which teacheth my hands to war and my fingers to fight."

The confidence of his townsmen was ever manifest by placing him in important positions. In 1820 he was a member of the Convention for the Revision of the State Constitution. In 1829 he was, by choice of the General Court, a member of the Executive Council.

In 1832 he was appointed to an important position in the Boston Custom House, in which office he continued for several years, fully sustaining his character for integrity and industry.

As a Christian he was faithful to his profession from his early conversion "to the end." The writer cannot speak particularly of his labors while in Lynn. He has, however, known him most intimately for nearly twenty years. He has seen him beloved and venerated by his large and respectable family. He has seen him honored as a worthy patriarch in the neighborhood where he resided. He has seen the trustees of the church looking to him as their head for wisdom to guide them in the time of peril. He has seen him in the official board, as steward and leader, the man of counsel, enterprise, and true courage. He .has seen him the persevering and endearing Sabbath-school Superintendent; he has seen him the devoted instructor of the Bible class, displaying the treasures of truth to those who would know the deep things of grace. He has seen him constant at church, faithful in improving all the means of grace, and faithful in the performance of all his duties. But he never did see a blemish upon his character; he never heard a word of reproach concerning him either as a man or a Christian.

For the last few years of his life, Father Mudge was afflicted with paralysis, which unfitted him for business and disabled him for service in the church. But he still loved the place where God's people assembled. He was often there with his smiling face, drinking freely at the fountain of life. He still loved the meetings of the official board, and of the trustees; and, although relieved of responsibility, would be present as an amateur.

He continued to totter about the streets in his vicinity, greeting the people with his pleasant salutation; and although his stricken tongue was not like the pen of a ready writer, he had a happy facility for saying, " God bless you."

For many months before his decease, he was aware of his peculiar liability to sudden death, and, as he said, " he kept his mind in heaven." He did, however, have notice of his departure. In the morning he ordered the collection of his family, and gave to each his wise counsel, his solemn injunction, and his final benediction.ᵃ At the going down of the sun he was gathered to the fathers, calm as the summer evening, filled with love, and in the full anticipation of a crown of glory, eternal and in the heavens.

Father Mudge became a member of the Wesleyan Association in 1835, when the "Zion's Herald" was supported by much labor and some pecuniary risk on the part of its members. But such a paper was requisite to the interests of the church, and on making his residence in Boston, he did not hesitate to join the "band of worthies" who had originated the enterprise and sustained the paper through many trials and adversities. In that band no man was more beloved and honored than he.

He lived to see this youthful object of his care become as a man rich in resources, commanding in influence, and wise in counsel. He lived to see the church which, in his childhood, was frail as the tender sapling, extend its branches from sea to sea, and over the whole breadth of the country; he lived to see the church of his choice, so feeble and despised in his youth, become the largest and most powerful in the nation. Such changes in the course of a life might well incline him to exclaim like Simeon, "Now, Lord, lettest thou thy servant depart in peace, for mine eyes have seen thy salvation."

OF THE SABBATH SCHOOL CHILDREN.

SARAH ELIZABETH, daughter of Charles Woodbury, died October 22, 1845, aged five years.

JOHN WESLEY, son of Mason Wheaton, died August 29, 1855, aged six years.

ELIZABETH SUTTON, daughter of James C. and Elizabeth Pearce, died Nov. 1, 1857, aged five years.

CHARLES B., son of Benjamin B. and Eleanor Hartford, died August 30, 1860, aged six years.

We have no record of the names, ages, or numbers of children which have died, members of our school. The above is all the data furnished in answer to a request from the pulpit. Some afflicted families have moved away, and quite a number of the children have belonged to families which did not attend our church. James G. Colman buried a daughter, some four or five years of age, in 1860. We well remember the affliction of Horace S. Favor and family, on the loss of a child about 1843.

We believe the first death in the school or congregation was that of Mary Ellen, a beautiful and interesting daughter of Ephraim C. Stowell, and sister of Charles A., aged four years and eight months. In the course of twenty-four years, perhaps as many as forty of these little lambs have been taken from our flock.

Softly lay your little heads
On their green and lowly beds;
Lovely flowers of every hue,—
Pearly tints and leaflets blue,—
On your little beds shall bloom,
Shedding fragrance round the tomb.

Sleep you, dearest; Jesus slept,
But an angel watch was kept!
O'er your Saviour's humble bed
Angel wings were nightly spread;
·Round his grave, at dawn of day,
Unseen harps their music play.

Jesus rose, and ye shall rise,
To that rest beyond the skies!
Even now, upon that shore,
Where your Saviour's gone before,
Faith beholds you, pure and bright,
With the elder sons of light.   MRS. MAXWELL.

OF YOUTH.

It would be impossible for us to form any opinion as to the number of persons who have died while members of, or after leaving the school. Of those belonging to the more permanent families, we have the names of Wm. B. and Harvey M., sons of Ezra Mudge; William, son of Noah Childs; Melissa, daughter of Joel Snow; Charles Wesley, son of Milton Gale; Mary Jane, daughter of James Wallace; Wm. J., son of James Drummond; Mrs. Mary (Studley) Gilbert, and Clarissa Knowles. We believe these were all exemplary and prayerful persons, and of them it may be said, "All is well." We suppose that no one of them left the school but to attend another on earth or in heaven. Some of them had removed to other schools. It was our design to publish some account of them; but we have already so far transgressed the limits assigned us that prudence forbids it. We have short notices of two early converts, and of one who had attended the school many years more than any of these.

CHARLES A., son of E. C. Stowell, was one of the original scholars of this school, and in Hannah M. Thompson's class. He was a noble boy. At the age of eight years he professed to enjoy the comforts of grace, having been blest in one of our meetings in March, 1838. We have known but little of him since he left the city. He graduated at Williams College and studied law. He went to Shasta, Cal., where he died of heart complaint about five years ago, at twenty-five years of age.

ROBERT, son of Isaac Rich, died February 18, 1844. He was not a member of our school, but attended our meetings in the time of a revival among the young people in the winter of 1838. He found peace in believing in one of the meetings at the school-room on Milton Street. At that time he was a member of the Bennet Street Sabbath School. In 1839, at the age of thirteen, he sustained a manly resolution in behalf of missions before the Juvenile Missionary Society. The resolution was seconded by Danforth S. Newcomb, another of the gems of the Bennet Street School, removed in 1854 to shine in a brighter sphere. Robert went with his parents to the Odeon. He was an active and efficient member of the Sabbath School. One of his last efforts was the delivery of a public Sabbath-school address at the Odeon. The address was well prepared and delivered by a natural and graceful orator. The loss of this only son was an intense family affliction, and one in which an extensive circle of friends deeply sympathized.

CHARLES HENRY, son of Charles and Relief L. Woodbury, died Oct. 11, 1853, aged 18 years.

We knew "Charlie" in those early days when he was "pleased with a rattle"; we remember his light curls and smiling face in the juvenile class; and the image of the youthful Charles Henry as he appeared in the Sabbath School, at church, at home, or on a visit, retains its full impression upon our vision. And still more vivid is the recollection of the solemn scene in that sad hour, when —

> "As a cloud of the sunset, slow melting in heaven,
> As a star that is lost when the daylight is given,
> As a glad dream of slumber which wakens in bliss,
> He did pass to the world of the holy from this."

He was a good scholar, and had determined on a liberal education preparatory to a life of usefulness. He lacked but a few months of preparation for the University. He might have fitted for college in Boston, but the pleasures of home associations were relinquished for the benefit of Wilbraham's pure mountain air. And yet it was there that he sickened, and from thence that he returned home with a raging fever,— to die.

At four years of age, he entered the infant department of the school, and even then was in the habit of discussing at home the topics introduced in the school. He remained a member and constant attendant of the school for thirteen years and until he left for Wilbraham. He visited home and the school at every vacation. His last visit to the school was in August, 1853. He was unusually interested in the subject of religion. He was invited to address the school, which he had never done extempore. After a little hesitation, he arose and with much emotion, and almost as if under the inspiration of a presentiment said, " I am once more in my own Sabbath School among my friends and associates, where I first entered as an infant scholar, and where I received many impressions which have often afforded me much comfort while I have been away from you. As I survey these seats, I find many of them vacant, or occupied by strangers to me. Many absent ones have left you for a home not of this world. I shall leave you again to pursue my studies in a distant village, and perhaps never more to meet you here. But whatever may be our lot, I hope that you and I shall study the Scriptures and follow their precepts, so that we may be prepared to meet in heaven." After the first three days of his sickness, he had but few lucid moments. These he improved in prayer. He had been a praying child from infancy, and "a child of prayer." He had been trained in the way he should go, and he delighted to remain therein.

Charles Henry was a favorite with his acquaintances, and he had many. The church, filled on a secular day with mourning friends from Wilbraham, from the city schools, and from the church and Sabbath school to perform their last sad offices, was a token of the estimation in which he was held. The death of such a "first-born" was a severe family affliction, not yet forgotten. It seems a mysterious providence, — but, hush: "The Lord gave, and the Lord hath taken away; blessed be the name of the Lord."

" The air is full of farewells to the dying,
    And mournings for the dead ;
  The heart of Rachel, for her children crying,
    Will not be comforted !

" Let us be patient ! The severe afflictions
    Not from the ground arise,
  But oftentimes celestial benedictions
    Assume this dark disguise.

" We see but dimly through the mists and vapors ;
    Amid these earthly damps
  What seem to us but sad, funereal tapers
    May be heaven's distant lamps.

" There is no Death ! What seems so is transition.;
    This life of mortal breath
  Is but a suburb of the life elysian,
    Whose portal we call Death !

                                    LONGFELLOW.

CHAPTER XV

MRS. MARY H. MAXWELL. — Among those who deserve honorable mention in this history, the name of Mrs. Maxwell stands conspicuous. In her pilgrimage she was, at two different periods, a teacher in our school. There are those who still remember her winning countenance and gentle manners, in both of which her uniform piety shone with a peculiar grace. Mrs. Maxwell was a lady of more than ordinary talent. She possessed sound, practical sense, keen perception, ready wit, and that rare discrimination, which leads to the discovery of small grains of precious metal, either mental or moral in its grosser surroundings. Hence what would seem a charity towards the weak was with her the result of a just appreciation of character. She united with the Methodist Episcopal Church in Portland, at the age of fifteen, and ever after maintained a consistent Christian life. There were painful passages, dark and mysterious, in her life, in which her friends looked on and trembled for her transparent character, but like the fining pot for gold were those trials to her soul, exalting, purifying, and refining her whole nature. The disease which terminated her earthly existence was most excruciating, which she bore with almost superhuman patience.

While undergoing a severe surgical operation at the McLean Hospital, she inhaled chloroform, and while insensible and paralyzed in every limb, her active spirit gave energy to the tongue, and she broke forth in the triumphant language of the Apostle, — "For I am persuaded, that neither death, nor life, nor angels, nor principalities, nor powers, nor things present, nor things to come, nor height, nor depth, nor any other creature, shall be able to separate us from the love of God which is in Christ Jesus our Lord." This outburst was so uncommon and so appropriate, that all were filled with admiration. She died in Shrewsbury, Mass., where she had been taken for the benefit of her health, in January, 1853, and in the thirty-ninth year of her age.

About the time she united with the church, her new-born soul gave theme to her poëtic pen. She was the admired and unknown " Mary " of the Maine Wesleyan Journal. Among her productions in that paper was the " Missionary's Farewell," addressed to Rev. G. F. Cox, as by his brother Rev. Melville B. Cox, on the occasion of his sailing for Liberia.

She wrote some for the Maine Wesleyan Journal, Zion's Herald, Sabbath School Messenger, Guide to Holiness, and largely for the Boys and Girls Magazine, during the four years in which this editor was Mark Forrester.

She might have stood beside the novelists of the day, a successful competitor for the prize of public favor and pecuniary independence ; but with Christian fidelity she resisted the temptation, and with holy zeal laid her rare gifts upon the altar of consecration to the cause of Sabbath Schools.

Her productions are still with us, and though dead, she still speaketh out of nearly one hundred Sabbath-school books. The entire Supplement to the Sunday School Harmonist, published by the Methodist Book Concern, and comprising one hundred and seven hymns, was composed by her. She was also the author of seven of the seventy-nine hymns in the Supplement to our church hymn-book, a larger number than is credited to any other individual. In these she will yet speak in the swelling song of millions. We have never been able to collect a complete list of Mrs. Maxwell's works. No matter ; their names and influence have a record, and she weareth her laurels in the presence of immortals.

Her career had an early close ; her labors were soon ended, and in an humble grave, in a neighboring village, reposes her precious dust. The grass annually freshens and withers over her grave where no kindred drops a tear, but the " Word of God," which lighted her pathway to the tomb, "endureth forever."

BENJ. H. BARNES died in Chelsea, April 18, 1858, aged 43 years. Mr. Barnes's employment, from a youth to near the close of life, was that of a bank officer, in which capacity he commanded the esteem and confidence of the business community.

He was principally indebted to Sabbath School instruction for his early knowledge of Christ. At the age of six years, he was so marked in his attention to Sabbath School duties as to be honored by the school and the pastor with the reception of a silver medal. At the age of fifteen, while a member of the Bennet Street Sabbath School, he gave his heart to Christ.

At nineteen he was a class leader; at twenty-one a steward. He remained a prominent member of the Bennet Street Church till 1837, when he left it to be one of the pioneers at North Russell Street. While here, he was active and useful in the Church and Sabbath School. When he thought he could be spared, he returned to Bennet Street Church, but soon left it to engage in a new religious enterprise in Chelsea, where he remained efficient and beloved till he joined the church triumphant. He was Treasurer of the Preachers' Aid Society, of the New England Conference, New England Wesleyan Education Society, Boston Young Men's Missionary Society, and of the Boston Wesleyan Association.

He was a local preacher of good talents, which he improved to the extent of his physical ability, and to the gratification of his hearers. He was precise in all his doings, and punctual in all his engagements. If he accepted an office he attended to its duties. He was on hand at the appointed time, and did not like to wait for tardy associates. We know of an incident appropriate here. Some twenty years ago, when he was an officer of the Boston Young Men's Missionary Society, a meeting of the Board was appointed to make arrangements for the anniversary meetings at all the Methodist Churches in Boston. The night was very stormy, but Mr. Barnes came all the way from Chelsea. Instead of meeting twelve or fifteen men, he found only the President. Should they get wet for nothing? Not a bit of it. The constitution did not prescribe the number for a quorum. The brothers went to work; the time for all the meetings was fixed; all the speakers selected; and all necessary arrangements concluded, to the unanimous satisfaction of the meeting. Everything was duly recorded, excepting the list of absentees, and a programme published, which met with general approbation.

The two brothers had their secret together for a long time, and occasionally exchanged congratulations on their ability to do two evenings' work in one, when left alone. Mr. Barnes was deeply interested in all the religious, moral, and literary movements of the times.

He was a decided anti-slavery man in the church, and a prominent member of the Liberty party, when it required great decision of character for a man in his position to take such a stand. He was an ardent lover and a generous supporter of the missionary cause. His pastor did well in saying that "he studied his missionary chart, as the merchant studies commerce." He frequently visited neighboring congregations to deliver addresses in behalf of missions, which were effective, as well-chosen words from a generous soul are sure to be.

The Boston Wesleyan Association, of which he had been a member for twenty-one years, passed a series of resolutions, relative to Mr. Barnes. We quote one of them, to which there will be a ready response by all who knew him.

"*Resolved*, That we shall ever cherish the memory of Brother Barnes's devotion, integrity, consistency, and purity of life, as a beautiful exemplification of the Christian religion, and as affording to surviving friends the most confident assurance of his blissful immortality."

JOSIAH RICHARDSON, of the Harvard Street Methodist Episcopal Church, Cambridge, died April 5, 1857, aged 46 years. We learn from an obituary by Rev. I. J. P. Collyer. that Mr. Richardson was converted in Maine about the year 1833. However that might have been, he made no pretensions to religious experience when he became a member of

our congregation. In the great revival in the winter of
1839–40, Mr. R. was very attentive to the meetings, but
delayed consecration for a long time, notwithstanding the
extreme interest of the meetings and many private personal
appeals. When he did yield, the good work was soon accomplished. The first time he started for the altar, he had pro-
ceeded but a few steps before he made the house ring
with his shouts of "Glory to God." He united with the
church through probation, and was a faithful member and
teacher, till his removal to Cambridge. For the remainder
of his history we quote Mr. Collyer, who says: "About
seventeen years since he removed to Cambridgeport, and
with steady perseverance he sustained by every possible
effort the interest of the church of his choice. Indeed, we
can hardly think of an important advance step in the church
in Cambridgeport, of which he was not the principal agent in
its accomplishment. Truly a good man has fallen. His tem-
perament was ardent, hence his religion was most fervent and
earnest. His sound judgment and practical knowledge gave
character to his piety and life, so that all who came within
the circle of his society found in him a judicious friend and
confident adviser. His loss will be felt by a large circle. The
church he has left can never find a more fervent and constant
friend. He was her largest pecuniary supporter, and was
almost always found in her prayer and class rooms, with a
warm and ready heart to carry forward the spiritual interests
of his Master. And he died just as we should expect such a
man to die, perfectly triumphant. To express his joy he said
to the writer: "It comes in floods I can't contain." To a
friend, he said, "I have been in heaven all day." This was
the last day of his life. His last message to his affectionate
and truly Christian mother was, "George, tell mother, Halle-
lujah," and these were his last words.

FRANCES ADELAIDE STUDLEY, the subject of this sketch,
was the daughter of John H. and Eliza W. Collins, and was
born in Goshen, Connecticut, April 23, 1827, where she resided, until her parents removed to Boston, in 1841. When

six years old, she gave good evidence of union in heart with
Christ. In her eleventh year she joined the Methodist Episcopal Church, in her native place. This step was not the
result of undue urging on the part of her friends, but a vol-
untary act, growing out of a fixed purpose to be a Christian;
and though some people may have entertained fears that one
so young did not appreciate, fully, the importance of such a
step, yet, from that time till her death, she maintained an
exemplary Christian character.

From her earliest childhood she was a diligent student of
nature, as well as of books. Her intellectual powers were
early developed. At the age of eleven, she wrote the
following.

THE DYING ROSE.

I heard a sigh, a mournful sigh,
  Come from a dying rose;
It spoke, and soon I heard it say,
  " My life is near its close.

" Once on my parent stem I grew,
  A lovely, smiling flower,
And little thought I then, that e'er
  O'er me dark clouds should lower.

" One morning, when the rising sun
  In matchless beauty shone,
A sudden storm broke off my stalk,
  And hither I was blown.

" For three long days I've languished here;
  I have not long to stay;
Hear then, my last, my dying words:
  ' Oh, trust not in to-day!'"

Then ceased its dying strains, and soon
  The floweret was no more;
But in my mind its precepts wise
  I shall forever store.

In her fugitive compositions, from which we have selected
the above, we not only detect her early thoughtfulness, but
we see the maturity of her Christian principle and feeling.
The sentiments which she expressed in these writings were
not the mere utterances of a poetic fancy; they were the
spoken experiences of an earnest, Christian heart.

During her fourteenth year, a little incident occurred which serves to show her earnestness and sincerity as a Christian. Her sister, waking from sleep one night, missed Frances from the room, and aroused her parents. Their anxiety was soon relieved by finding her in the sitting-room of the family. She said that she had been wakeful in the night, and as she had some doctrinal doubts which perplexed her mind, she had gone away by herself, and read the entire Epistle of Paul to the Romans. This was characteristic of her. She did her own thinking in those important matters which relate to the soul.

In her eighteenth year, she was appointed an associate teacher in one of the public grammar schools of Boston. She knew but few idle moments in the interval of school hours. Without neglecting the courtesies of social life, or omitting her stated religious duties, she mastered the French language, so as to speak it fluently and with great accuracy, and made very considerable progress in German and Italian. Her course of English reading was both extensive and thorough. It embraced divinity, ethics, poetry, and general literature. Few so young, have read so much; and fewer still, whether young or old, retain so much of what they read. In addition to her daily duties as teacher, she was an officer of various benevolent societies, an instructor in an evening school for adults, a Sunday-school teacher, and a frequent contributor, with her pen, to the interests of education. She was actively engaged in the North Russell Street Sabbath School, during a period of nine years.

In September, 1850, she was married to Rev. William S. Studley, then pastor of the Methodist Episcopal Church in Malden, Mass. In her intercourse with society as a pastor's wife, she was always unobtrusive, but never diffident. She seemed to fear, rather than court applause; yet when it came, she could meet it with surpassing grace and modesty. She was ever the same unassuming person, whether in the company of the cultivated or ignorant: never boastful of her accomplishments, yet always ready to lend the charm of her endowments to every circle in which she moved.

In the month of October, 1851, she gave birth to a daughter, and from that time her health steadily declined; but in the midst of wasting energies, there was no complaint or murmur. Her faith in Christ triumphed. She died on the 26th of December, 1851. Her father, in imprinting his last kiss upon her pallid lips, said, My daughter, you are almost home. She replied, "Yes, dear father, I wish I was there." She then observed that she had given everything into the hands of her Saviour, with whom she cheerfully trusted all. When she was so weak that she could only whisper, she expressed her full confidence in Christ as a Saviour. In the closing hour, she sunk rapidly and spoke but little. Her last words, twice repeated, were: "God take me! God take me!" And he did take her to be one of his angel worshippers, "in that divine abode," where

> " Change finds no pathway, memory no dark trace;
> And oh, bright victory! death and sin no place."

In all the relations of life,—as a daughter, teacher, wife, friend,—she manifested the humble, self-denying, yet cheerful spirit of a true Christian believer.

> " Not upon her heart, now, the solemn angel
> Hath evil wrought;
> Her funeral anthem is a glad evangel : —
> The good die not! "

NOAH CHILDS died in 1849. He is mentioned elsewhere as one of the primitive members of this church, and one of the first stewards. He was at one time teacher of a Bible class. He was a man of feeble health, but he attended faithfully to the duties appropriate to any station which he consented to fill. He was a quiet man, and of few words. His time was much devoted of necessity to his secular business; he trained his children in the way they should go; and endeavored to "live in peace with all men." In his life, and in his death, the words of the Psalmist were verified. "Great peace have they that love thy law."

Sylvanus W. Robinson died in September, 1849. Mr. Robinson was the teacher of a Bible class in this school. He was an attorney-at-law. We had much to hope from him and his family, but were destined to disappointment. After he had been with us a few months, a fatal disease fastened upon him. He returned to his home in Maine, where, after a protracted illness, he departed this life in great peace, and the sure hope of eternal life in the better land.

Rev. Amos P. Battey, at one time a member of North Russell Street Church, and teacher in the Sabbath School, pursued his studies in view of the ministry, at Kent's Hill, Maine. He joined the Maine Conference in 1841, and died October 9, 1849.

The General Minutes say truly, " Brother Battey was a good man, a pious Christian, a devoted minister, and a faithful pastor of the church of God. His time, talents, and property were all spent in his Master's service. His last and dying effort in the pulpit was made in Hampden, several months before his death. His text was Phil. iii. 21 : ' Who shall change our vile body, that it may be fashioned like unto his glorious body, according to the working whereby he is able to subdue all things unto himself.' His message was delivered in demonstration of the Spirit, and in power, for he spoke like a dying man to dying men. Sighs, tears, and praises mingled in every part of the congregation. That evening he bled again at the lungs ; and while the blood was flowing freely, one expressed regret that he had preached that day, to which he replied, ' I shall never regret it, if I die to-night. My work is now done.' He preached no more. As he went slowly down to the grave, the doctrine of the resurrection was his all-inspiring theme. The day of his death he was able to walk about his premises, but was attacked suddenly with hemorrhage from the lungs, and died sitting in his chair. We doubt not he reigns on high, where we hope soon to meet him."

HANNAH M. THOMPSON was the daughter of Ebenezer and Hannah Thompson. She had a very cheerful and happy disposition, a brilliant imagination, a thorough education, and, to sanctify and direct the whole, she was deeply pious. She loved her friends dearly, and the affection was sweetly reciprocated.

She was one of the first teachers in our Sabbath School, and one of the best. She wrote freely such articles as were needed for school examinations and exhibitions. She wrote extensively for the Sabbath School Messenger, and some for the Guide to Holiness, and other periodicals. She was the author of two interesting Sabbath School books, several editions of which were published, " Procrastination," and " The Widow's Jewels."

In 1838, Miss Thompson, with much diffidence, accepted an invitation to become Preceptress of the Wilbraham Academy, — a position which she sustained with brilliant success till the fall of 1841, when she was united in marriage with Rev. Humphrey Pickard, D.D., principal of the Mount Allison Academy, Sackville, N. B. While in Sackville, she labored diligently in her Master's cause, was honored by society, and endeared to the students. She was a devoted and cherished wife, and the mother of two children.

She died in March, 1844. Mr. Pickard wrote : " Her death was in a moment, and utterly unlooked for by us. So unlike death did it seem that we could not entirely give her up for several hours."

A book embracing her history, diary, correspondence, and some of her other writings, was published in Boston. It was admirably edited by her sister's husband, Rev. E. Otheman. We have long felt that this work ought to be republished. We are aware that the title, " Memoirs," is unpopular ; but it might with propriety have another name, or, with the present, be " noticed " into a reputation. With its chaste literary merit, its truly poetic style, and deep-toned piety, it could not fail of a high appreciation.

Mrs. Julia C. Hascall, wife of Rev. Jefferson Hascall, died Aug. 6, 1842, aged 30 years.

During her two years' connection with this church, Mrs. Hascall labored faithfully as a pastor's wife, and became much endeared to the people. She was associate teacher with Miss Mary Ann Lewis in the infant school, a position for which she was peculiarly qualified, and which she sustained with eminent success.

We can indorse the sentiments of her biographer, who said—

"She was a friend and companion of no ordinary worth. Possessed of a mind at once lively yet candid, brilliant yet grave, her conversation was of a peculiar zest. In her manners, timid yet self-possessed, easy yet unaffected, and evincing withal a peculiar sweetness of temper, she was the admiration of the circle in which she moved. But these were not the chief of her excellences; for in that casket might be found the confiding heart, and in that heart the pure aroma of friendship. * * * As a minister's wife she was always devoted to her work. Having thrown herself upon the altar of the itinerancy, nothing could be more painful to her feelings than the thought of withholding that sacrifice, even for a moment. In this sphere of action, her course was short but brilliant. How many souls she had been the means of alluring to Christ, her well-gemmed crown alone can tell."

Her last sickness was of many months' duration, in which she was patient, peaceful, cheerful, and resigned ; in her own words,—"I feel that I am in the arms of my Saviour, and all is safe." Her farewell charge was, "Be faithful, be faithful."

Mrs. Hascall and Mrs. King were as one soul the two years they were together, and they both anticipated an early union in heaven. We find in Mrs. King's scrap-book, these lines :—

TO JULIA.

Rest, gentle spirit, rest!
Thy conflicts o'er, thy labors done, —
Angels thy friends ; thy home,
The presence of the Holy One.

I want to go and view
The glories of thy pure abode ;
With thee to love and live,
Forever, EVER with our God.

Mrs. Nancy B. King died Nov. 23, 1846, aged 39 years. Though Mrs. King designed from the commencement to embark in the new enterprise, she remained a while at the Bennet Street Church out of sympathy with an interesting Bible class of young ladies. She became connected with this church, and during her whole membership was a faithful and successful teacher. She usually had a large class of young ladies, who left to be teachers as occasion required. Though of a retiring disposition, she shunned no duty in any of the meetings of the church, or of the several societies of which she was a member.

In 1845, providence directed her ways to the Odeon, and thence to Bromfield Street Church, of which she was a member at her decease, but North Russell Street remained her specially beloved church.

She was a writer of more than ordinary capacity, and contributed freely but anonymously to the pages of Zion's Herald, Sabbath School Messenger, and Guide to Holiness. She left a volume of miscellaneous papers in manuscript, but with the injunction that they should not be published.

The development of a scirrhous tumor in the spring of 1846 rendered the near and sudden approach of death certain. She had this assurance from a council of physicians about three months before her death. Of the state of her mind during this period, Rev. J. T. Pettee said truly : " She not only bore up with heroic fortitude against the last approaches of death, but rose in triumph, and shouted victory above them. Such a scene of triumph I was hardly prepared to witness. The gate of death itself was a triumphal arch to our departing sister, and the dark valley a triumphal way to heaven. But words are inadequate to any just description of the scene. Those only who have seen the saints ascend to glory, ' made perfect through suffering,' like the Captain of their salvation, can know it."

One of her last efforts was to write the following address. We deem it appropriate for the close of this work :—

To my Beloved Christian Friends :—

Through the tender mercy of our heavenly Father, I am permitted, though in weakness, to address you a few words of comfort and of admonition, and with them my last testimony to the worth of religion, and of the preciousness of the Saviour, and of the comforting hope, that, through the mercy of God, and the atonement of the adorable Redeemer, I shall be saved.

Wonderful to my mind is the plan of redemption,— unspeakable the compassion of Jesus towards a sinful race! The language of mortals is too poor to convey any proper idea of the great reality.

But, my dear brothers and sisters, the eye of faith beholds that country where the plan of salvation appears to its inhabitants ten thousand times more glorious; where the beauteous brightness of the infinite Saviour is the centre of all attraction; and though the language spoken be the language of immortals, and full of heavenly meaning, yet through eternity the song of redemption will be the unceasing song, still new, and increasingly glorious.

From this world of glory the infinite Saviour looks down on his toiling, trusting followers, and lovingly invites them to cast their cares upon him, assuring them that he careth for them, and is touched with pity for their distresses.

I rejoice, dear friends, that this Saviour is mine, that he blesses me with his presence, and comforts me with his love.

He is to me the chiefest among ten thousands, and the one altogether lovely; and though I have nothing to bring to him but vileness, he imparts to me his grace, and with it the assurance that he will not leave me in this last great extremity. No earthly friend can pass with me through death's fearful valley, but I believe that the light of my Saviour's countenance will be my comfort there.

The few remaining days of my earthly sojourn will doubtless be days of suffering; but I know that, however severe, they will be lighter than I deserve; this I can leave to the direction of divine wisdom. I am taught that the heavenly purifier sits by the furnace, — that he takes not his eye from the silver until he beholds reflected therein his own image.

How comforting the thought that God, the holy God, condescends to take away our dross, and give us his own pure image.

How full of comfort is the Christian's journey. If he belong to Christ, he may feel that all things belong to him, that he who spared not his own Son will with him freely give us all things. What could we ask for more? — everything for our good on earth and eternal rest in heaven. I am looking forward to this blessed rest with anticipations of delight, and though all unworthiness, I believe that Jesus will at last bring me to the mansion he has prepared for me.

And now, dear brethren and sisters, farewell. Live near to God; seek to be led in all things by the divine Spirit; love the blessed Bible more; love the souls of sinners more, and in the work of saving souls follow closely in the footsteps of the Lord; love the closet and all the means of grace; love Christians; be humble; remember how dear to the Saviour is each member of his body, and while you seek in all things to glorify God, he will bless your labors; he will make his grace abound to you in all things, and be himself your portion and reward.

I have sometimes thought I should love to be with you again in class, if it was the will of heaven; but I submit without a murmur. The room where you so often meet has been to me a sanctuary; and some of you, dear sisters, can testify how sweet have been the visits of the Saviour in that place of prayer.

Again, I must say farewell. We meet no more on earth; but I trust, as one and another finish their work, having fought the good fight and kept the faith, there will be administered to them an abundant entrance into the everlasting kingdom of our God and Redeemer.

TABLE OF STATISTICS TO JANUARY 22, 1861.

Date.	Pastors.	Superintendents.	Church Members.	Officers and Teachers.	Scholars.	Books in Library.
1838	Moses L. Scudder	Albert H. Brown.......	114	28	106	300
1839 .	Moses L. Scudder......	Albert H. Brown	164	30	116	....
1840	Jefferson Hascall	Dexter S. King	316	42	191	437
1841	Jefferson Hascall.......	Dexter S. King	310	44	245	445
1842	Charles K. True........	Ezra Mudge	430	37	225	....
1843	Charles K. True........	Joshua B. Holman......	320	26	163	560
1844	George Landon........	John H. Collins	320	28	98	560
1845	George Landon	Daniel Warren	290	45	120	....
1846	William H, Hatch	Daniel Warren..........	226	36	128	....
1847	William H. Hatch	John H. Collins	200	41	139	550
1848	William Rice...........	Franklin Rand	213	40	155	350
1849	William Rice ...:.......	Luther L. Tarbell	235	36	201	550
1850	Mark Trafton...........	Luther L. Tarbell	257	35	206	....
1851	Mark Trafton..:......,..	Luther L. Tarbell	199	37	219	....
1852	Nelson E. Cobleigh	Luther L. Tarbell	270	42	308	1,100
1853	Nelson E. Cobleigh.....	Luther L. Tarbell	292	38	294	.....
1854	J. Augustus Adams....	Moses W. Merrill	294	32	260	....
1855	J. Augustus Adams	Alden Avery............	275	39	230	....
1856	Moses A. Howe	Moses W. Merrill.......	248	31	205	....
1857	William S. Studley	Luther L. Tarbell	255	38	265	....
1858	Henry W. Warren.....	Luther L. Tarbell	283	46	261	922
1859	Henry W. Warren.....	The Pastor.............	305	39	281	....
1860	J. W. Dadmun	J. Fred Eastman	325	40	297	950
1861	J. W. Dadmun	J. Fred Eastman	360	46	353	....

In the above Table, the date shows the time of taking the numbers in the Church and School, but it refers to the closing of each year's service of the Pastors and Superintendents, the first appointments having been made in 1837.

The numbers in the Church are as reported for the General Minutes, and the Statistics of the School, as they were prepared for its Annual Report.

J. B. Holman was Superintendent from January to April in 1842. William S. Studley was Superintendent from March to July in 1844, when he left the city in pursuit of an education. Alden Avery succeeded him, holding office one month, when he resigned, and moved away from this part of the city.

MEMBERS OF THE NORTH RUSSELL ST. CHURCH

FROM JANUARY 22, 1837, TO JANUARY 22, 1861.

Abbott, Phebe 1841	*Babb, Eliza 1841	*Bellows, Sarah........1840
Abbott, Rosetta.......1844	Badger, Ann Matilda .1840	*Berry, Ann M.........1841
†Adair, Eliza 1849	Bagley, Perkius H....1838	Beverly, Eunice S....1837
*†Adaly, Ann...........1854	Bailey, Jonas M......1847	*Beverton, Charles.....1853
†Adaly, Mary.........1852	Bailey, Lydia.........1847	*Beverton, Mrs........1853
*Adams, Ann..........1847	Bailey, Amos..........1848	*Bickford, Abigail 1842
*Adams, Ann M. 1841	*†Banfield, Mary........1840	†Binney, Isabella H. ...1859
*Adams, Emily 1840	*†Banfield, Ann 1841	Binney, Sarah 1839
*Adams, Eliza A.	Baker, Mary A........1850	Binner, Mary A.......1858
(Saunders)......1837	*Baker, Martha A......1850	*Birchsted, Ann E. 1852
Adams, Mary 1840	*†Baker, M. A. (Mudge).1852	*Bird, Daniel S.........1840
Adams, Mary A.......1847	†Baker, Mary A........1852	Blaisdale, Ruth A.....1841
Adams, Samuel 1837	Baker, Thankful R. ...1853	*Blair, Jane 1854
*Adams, Sarah J......1844	*Baker, Henry.........1854	*†Blakemore, Amanda
Adams, Sophia M. ...1853	†Baker, John 1855	(Hancock) 1853
Adams, Temperance ..1839	†Baker, Martha 1859	*†Blakemore, John E. ..1853
†Alexander, James ...1857	*Balcom, John A.......1841	Blakemore, Letitia....1853
Aldrich, H. A.........1851	*Ball, Nancy (Thom) ..1850	*Blakemore, Letitia B..1855
Allen, Elizabeth A....1840	*†Baldwin, Betsey 1859	Blakemore, William ..1853
†Allen. Esther 1850	Barnes, Benj. H.......1837	*†Blaney, Arabella C. ..1860
Allen, Fanny 1845	*Barnard, Eliza........1841	*Blaney, Charles W. ..1842
*†Almy, H. A. (Lewis) ..1838	Barnard, Alsa 1847	*Blaney, Ann C........1852
Andrews, Elizabeth...1841	Barron, Benj. T........1849	*†Blodgett, Sarah J. 1852
Andros, Martha C. ...1853	Barron, Ann H. 1849	*†Bodge, Noah..........1840
Apline, Adaline.......1839	*†Bartlett, Gertrude J.	*†Bodge, Adeline S. 1852
*Appleton, Sarah E. ..1853	(Collins) 1850	Bolton, Sarah 1852
†Appleton, Thomas....1854	†Basford, Jerusha......1843	*Bonney, Mary C......1840
Armstrong, Cath. S. ..1843	Basford, Sarah........1845	Bovyer, Frances M. ...1853
*Ashley, Luke 1838	Battey, Amos P. 1839	Bovyer, John 1850
Ashley, Mary B. 1838	Bates, Joanna..........1840	*Bovyer, Samuel.......1852
*†Athern, Josephine V..1840	Bates, Sarah 1841	*Bovyer, Joanna.......1852
Atherton, Julia.......1838	Bates, Eleazer.........1843	Boyce, Mary Ann.....1852
†Atkins, Helen A.......1860	Bates, Eliza 1847	Boyce, Jacob..........1852
*†Atkins, Freeman S. ...1858	Beal, Christopher 1851	Booth, Walker 1842
*†Atwood, Sarah S......1853	*Beal, Mary...........1842	*Bosworth, Geo. W.....1838
*†Atwood, Harriet......1853	Beaman, Eri B. 1845	Bosworth, Cath. F.....1837
*†Atwood, Augusta A...1853	Beaman, Rosanna.....1845	*Bosworth, Dorothea ..1848
†Atwood, Hannah 1851	Bean, Susan E.........1855	*Boss, Charles.........1840
*†Atwood, Osmyn.......1860	Beckwith, Elvira......1845	Bowers, Olive.........1839
Atkinson, Emeline....1839	Beckwith, Augusta ...1851	Bowers, Rebecca.....1842
Atkinson, Hannah 1842	*Beckwith, A. J........1850	Bowers, Julia Ann....1844
Avery, Alden 1844	Beeching, Richard....1849	*Boynton, Moses.......1838
Avery, Helen W.......1852	Beeching, Eliza 1849	*Boynton, Thais M.....1833
Avery, Lucinda M.....1844	Beecher, Sarah.......1850	*Boynton, Samuel 1838
*†Ayer, Hannah 1852	Bellows, Mary P......1839	*Boyer, Fred...........1854

*From Probation.   † Present Member.

MEMBERS OF THE NORTH RUSSELL STREET SABBATH SCHOOL,

JANUARY 22, 1861.

OFFICERS.

J. FRED EASTMAN,	- -	*Superintendent;*
D. W. GARDNER,	- -	*Assistant Superintendent;*
SUSAN E. DAMRELL,	- -	*Female Assistant Superintendent;*
CHARLES A. PATCH,	- -	*Secretary;*
E. B. HINE,	- -	*Treasurer;*
WILLIAM E JACKSON,	-	*Librarian;*
O. P. MERRITT,	- -	*First Assistant Librarian;*
RICHARD PATTEE,	- -	*Second " "*
CHARLES WALKER,	- -	*Third " "*
JULIA A. WHEATON,	- -	*Organist.*

TEACHERS.

MALE.	FEMALE.
T. Warren,	Augusta Atwood,
Edgar Webb,	Gallah Levi,
D. W. Russell,	Jane Levi,
R. B. Graham,	Isabella Welch,
F. S. Atkins,	Sarah E. Lewis,
J. S. Damrell,	Minnie J. Leavitt,
O. F. French,	Mary F. Greenleaf,
A. G. West,	Eliza H. Waitt,
J. R. Sumner,	Nella J. Foss,
W. H. Crockett,	Julia A. Gardner,
T. J. Tucker, Jr.,	Harriet A. Clayton,
A. J. Beckwith,	Mercy A. Goodrich,
W. S. Kyle,	Maria E. Tucker,
B. Hinds,	Laura M. Eastman,
G. S. Butrick,	Jane Hopkirk,
T. N. Chase,	Elizabeth Warren,
Adams Perry, } Substitute	Harriet Sawyer,
Isaac Pierce, } Teachers.	Harriet Pinkham,

SCHOLARS.

Abbott, G.	Babbitt, L. C.	Bruce, Frank
Adams, Anna	Badger, Caroline	Brey, S. A.
Almy, Hattie E.	Badger, Abbie	Bullard, L.
Alders, Lavina	Badger, F.	Burrill, Viola
Anderson, L. B.	Barnum, Sarah	Butrick, Laura
Appleton, Thomas	Beal, Mary	Burnham, J. A.
Appleton, Thomas R.	Beal, Anna	Bowker, Lottie
Appleton, George J.	Blaney, Arabella C.	
Atwood, Harriet N.	Blaney, Mary A.	Caldwell, M. A.
Atwood, Osmyn H.	Blodgett, Sarah J.	Carter, M.
Atkins, Mrs. Helen	Brown, James	Chase, U.

Chesley, Ida
Cheeney, George A.
Cilley, Clara
Clark, Amelia S.
Clark, Richard S.
Clayton, Henrietta
Coburn, Martha
Coburn, Etta
Collins, John H.
Collins, John W.
Cobb, Clara A.
Cobb, Harriet E.
Condry, Susan E.
Connut, Sarah S.
Couillard, Joseph H.
Cox, Eliza
Cunningham, Hattie A.
Cushman, E.
Cutter, Jane E.
Cutter, Mrs.
Cushing, L. V.
Cushing, William R.
Cushing, Joseph W.
Curtis, L. C.

Dadmun, L. A. E.
Dadmun, Marthaetta
Dadmun, Willietta
Dadmun, Charles W.
Davis, E. L.
Davis, Sarah M.
Doherty, Caroline M.
Doniger, Annie
Dormit, C. C.
Dyer, J. W P.

Eastman, Ermon D.
Eaton, Frances
Eichorn, Mary
Evans, Alice F.

Fairbanks, Isabella
Fairbanks, Ella
Farley, A. P.
Farley, Martha
Fawcett, Lizzie F.
Fisher, Laura F.
Foss, Ansel G.
Foster, W. F.
Foster, I. C.
Foster, Charles W.
Foster, Frank M.
Foster, M.
Follett, Mary
Fossett, Helen,
Foristall, Joseph
French, Z. H.
French, Eveline L.

Fuller, Sarah E.

Gould, H. A.
Gould, Arthur C.
Gould, Amelia S.
Gould, R. H.
Goulding Margaret G.
Goulding, Amelia
Goodrich, Sarah,
Goodrich, Lucy
Gordon, Emma A.
Graham, Mrs.
Greenleaf, George S.
Goddard, Emma

Harvey, Joseph R.
Harvey, Philip
Harding, I. R.
Harding, N. A.
Harding, P.
Harding, Osmond,
Harding. Emma,
Hall, Martha O.
Hall, A. N.
Hartford, Mary E.
Hartford, Mary,
Hatton, Isabella
Hayne, Clara J.
Heath, Henry
Head, Annie
Hine, A. J.
Hine, Mary C.
Hinds, Llewellyn B.
Hinds, Addie,
Hinds, F. K.
Higgins, Beriah,
Higgins, Philip
Holden, Kittie
Holmes, Julia
Houghton, Emma J.
Howes, Clara
Howes, Emma
Hopkins, Amelia B.
Hoyt, Hattie
Ingraham, W. H.

Jackson, E. F.
Jenkins, Annie B.
Jenkins, Susie B.
Johnson, R. N.
Johnson, Lizzie R.
Jones, William
Jones, M. H.
Jones, George R.
Josselyn, M. A.
Joy, Charles S.

Kenney, William C.

Keyes, E.
Kimball, Charles T. P.
Kyle, E. J.

Levi, William G.
Lincoln, Helen A.
Lowe, M.
Lowe, James
Longly, Mary N. H.
Longly, Edwin
Longly, M. A.
Longly, Harriet L.

Magrath, George
Magrath, Charles
Magrath, Etta
Mann, John
Mann, W. W.
Mason, Eunice E.
Martin, Martha B.
Martin, Solon D.
Maxwell, George B. F.
Maxwell, E. M.
Melvin, M. C.
Mellen, William
Merrill, Julia E.
Merritt, Charles H. jr.
McClannin, Joseph W.
Miles, Lucretia T.
Mitchell, Richard
Morse, John A.
Morse, Howard B.
Morse, M.
Morse, Emma F.
Morse, Martha
Morse, Sarah F.
Morse, Ellen
Morse, George M.
Montgomery, Margaret
Morton, U.
Morey, Elisha E.

Neal, A.
Newcomb, Lizzie
Newcomb, Helen
Newell, D. E.

Odenwald, F. L.

Patch, Caroline T.
Pattee, Mary
Perkins, E. F.
Pike, A. C.
Pike, Frank W.
Pinkerton, George F.
Pearce, Wesley
Pearce, C. E.
Pearce, James W.

Pollo, Edward
Perry, John F.

Rand, L.
Ranney, Charles F.
Reed, Joseph
Reed, Mrs.
Remick, Emma
Remick, A.
Rice, Martha A.
Richardson, Allen
Roach, Margaret
Rowe, Sarah
Robie, Frank E.
Rogers, J. O.
Russell, William
Russell, Frank
Russell, A.
Ruggles, Jennie
Ruggles, G. F.
Ruggles, Julia E.

Sawyer, Emily
Sawyer, J.
Sawtelle, Carrie R.
Schelleny, Mary P.
Simonds, Williemine
Skelton, Parker R.
Skimmings, Mary
Skimmings, C. E.
Skimmings, Marie
Skimmings, Charles H.
Skillings, Belle
Spaulding, J. C.

Spaulding, F. W.
Spaulding, E. H.
Spalding, J. R.
Spooner, A. E.
Spooner, Sidney
Spooner, Horace
Spooner, Emma L.
Spriggs, Mary L.
Stimson, Charles
Stimson, Frederic
Stimpson, Caroline
Stevens, George H.
St. John, Lizzie
Stokel, Charlotte
Stoddard, George W. F.
Stoddard, Georgianna
Smith, Georgianna
Smith, Florence J.
Snow, Mary
Studley, Rev. William S.

Taylor, Ruth
Taylor, Florilla
Thomas, Juliette B.
Todd, Samuel A.
Todd, Sarah
Tower, Daniel T.
Tracy, Adelaide E.
Tracy, W. E.
Tracy, A.
Trumbull, Nathaniel
Tubbs, Mary J.
Tucker, H. L.
Tuckett, William

Tuckett, Emma Y.
Tupper, Ella B.

Verney, Emma

Wadsworth, Alfred
Waitt, Maria L.
Waitt, Eliza L.
Waitt, Madeline
Ware, Albert C.
Warren, L.
Warren, George
Watson, Sarah C.
Webb, Paulina
Weed, Orison C.
Weeks, Joseph
Weeks, William
Weeks, Sarah B.
Wentworth, Frank P.
Wentworth, Charles H.
White, E. J.
Wheaton, Hattie B.
Widger, Emily
Williams, Eliza A.
Williams, Viola A.
Williams, Elvina E.
Woodbury, Carrie A.
Woodbury, Isabella A.
Woodbury, George A.
Woodbury, Eddie S.
Woodworth, Elizabeth
Woodworth, Lizzie
Wright, George
Wright, George F.

INFANT DEPARTMENT.

SUSAN E. DAMRELL—Teacher.

Almy, George W. Jr.

Babbitt, Martha L.
Bradford, Emma
Brown, James

Cavarero, Amelia C.

Dadmun, Lalleu
Damrell, Carrie Maria
Damrell, John E. S.
Davis, Mary E.
Drew, Cora J.
Dunkin, Mary B.

Denniger, Albert
Denniger, Emily

Evans, Ida B.
Farley, John E.
Farley, Frank H.
Fairbanks, John A.
Franklin, William

Gould, Waldo G.
Graham, Charles G.
Grows, Ella

Harding, Eva

Hammond, Hattie S.
Hinds, Josephine

Johnson, Lizzie R.

Kyle, Flavil W.

Lampher, Charles H.
Ledworth, Sarah S.
Lowe, John
Lowe, Willie

Merritt, Mary E.
Mitchell, Martha

Nichols, Addie

Osbourne, Frank S.

Parkins, Wilford N.
Pierce, Annie E.
Preble, Esther

Reed, Sarah C.
Robbins, George

Scott, Alice

Spencer, Charlotte L.
Spencer, Willie H.
Spencer, George W.
Smith, Frank A.
Smith, Georgiana
Smith, Maria
Stevens, Addie P.
Stetson, Lewis A.
Stover, Lizzie C.
Stover, Lillie E.

Tupper, Willie

Varney, Ada

Watson, E. C.
Watson, E. A.
Watson, S. J.
White, David
Willey, Martha A.
Willey, Mary E.
Willey, Eddie
White, Charles H.
Wright, Annie S.

The Secretaries have been: Thomas Patten, Jr., Harvey M. Mudge, J. W. Whitcomb, Benj. Cushing, Paul R. B. Pearson, Edward A. Pearson, Nath'l. Carr, J. K. C. Sleeper, Abram W. Rand, Russell J. Parker, Eben M. Tibbetts, Joseph H. Tucker, John E. Blakemore, A. J. Beckwith, Thomas J. Tucker.

These are not in chronological order, and there may have been others.

Our list of Treasurers and Librarians is so deficient that we omit the whole.

CONTENTS.

www.ingramcontent.com/pod-product-compliance
Lightning Source LLC
Chambersburg PA
CBHW060246030726

47493CB00025B/2740